Geronimo Stilton

THE HOUR OF MAGIC

THE EIGHTH ADVENTURE
IN THE
KINGDOM OF FANTASY

Scholastic Inc.

Library of Congress Cataloging-in-Publication Data available

ISBN 978-0-545-82336-4

Text by Geronimo Stilton
Original title *Ottavo Viaggio nel Regno della Fantasia*
Cover by Danilo Barozzi
Illustrations by Danilo Barozzi, Silvia Bigolin, Carla De Bernardi, and Piemme's Archives. Color by Christian Aliprandi.
Graphics by Chiara Cebraro and Yuko Egusa

Special thanks to Kathryn Cristaldi
Translated by Andrea Schaffer
Interior design by Kay Petronio

10 9 8 7 6   18 19 20 21 22

Printed in China   38
First edition, June 2016

The Band of Time Seekers

750L

Geronimo Stilton

I am the publisher of *The Rodent's Gazette*, the most famouse newspaper on Mouse Island. This is my eighth trip to the Kingdom of Fantasy!

Scribblehopper

I was Sir Geronimo of Stilton's first guide in the Kingdom of Fantasy. I am a literary frog with tons of ideas. Someday I will write a book!

Little Princess Buzzy

I am the niece of the queen of the bees, the third of the noble Buzzers. Some say I am high maintenance; I say so what! I am royalty, after all!

Queenie

I am Scribblehopper's cousin. I am part of the noble dynasty of the Greenbloods. I usually don't hang around commoners. Ribbit!

Solitaire

I am a knight who leads Geronimo through the Land of Time. I wear a mask over my face to keep my identity a secret. Shhh . . . I've got my reasons.

Dragon of Time

I'm an emerald-green dragon who is loyal and true. I am Geronimo's ride from the Land of Time.

Hee Haw

I am the court jester in the Land of Time. I love to ruffle Geronimo's fur! Hee haw!

SNIFF! SNIFF!

That morning, when I stuck my **snout** out the window of my office, I noticed that the air had a special **smell**. It smelled like it was about to **snow**! Oh, how I love snowy winters in New Mouse City, my home sweet home!

Oops, I'm sorry, I forgot to introduce myself. My name is Stilton, *Geronimo Stilton*. I have

Sniff! Sniff!

brown fur and glasses, and I am the publisher of *The Rodent's Gazette*, the most **famouse** newspaper on Mouse Island.

Anyway, as I was saying, that day in New Mouse City, I could tell snow was on the way. I was so excited! Don't get me wrong: I'm not a big fan of **FREEZING** weather or heavy-duty shoveling, but have you ever seen the city under a blanket of snow? Let me tell you — there is nothing more beautiful! Plus, when it snows, I love to go **sledding** with my dear nephew Benjamin and warm my paws with a cup of hot cheese by the fire.

I was still dreaming about hot cheese when the phone rang. **Riiinnng**!

It was my grandfather William Shortpaws, who boomed, "Grandson, have

Grandsooon!

GRANDFATHER
WILLIAM SHORTPAWS,
founder of
The Rodent's Gazette

you finished writing the book?" When I didn't respond immediately, Grandfather screeched, "Have you **forgotten**?! You need to write the new *Kingdom of Fantasy* book! It's due next week!"

I hit my forehead with my paw. Rats! How had I forgotten?! Of course, I couldn't tell my **RAGING** grandfather this, so I said, "Don't worry, Grandfather. I already have the whole **book** in my head — sort of — and lots of good ideas . . ."

What my grandfather doesn't understand is that in order to write about the Kingdom of Fantasy, I have to **GO** there. On a recent trip, Queen Blossom gave me a magical sapphire ring that would let me visit whenever I wanted. Unfortunately, I had misplaced it! The only other way to get there is by **dreaming**.

"Remember that this is the most important

book of the year, and readers are waiting **impatiently**. Do you understand, Grandson?" Grandfather William went on.

Then, before I could hang up, he added, "Oh, and by the way, we're all coming to your house tonight to **celebrate** Aunt Sweetfur's birthday, understand?"

I hurried to squeak. "Of course! Certainly!"

Worried (not about the birthday but about the book I had forgotten to write), I left my office and headed home. I hoped that taking a walk would fill me with **ideas**, but my mind was blank.

As I walked, I noticed the most delicious aromas. First I passed by Squeakini's, my favorite bakery in the city, and smelled their **warm cheese donuts**. Yum!

I bought a box to serve that evening for Aunt Sweetfur's birthday. Naturally, I had to

taste a donut to make sure they were fresh. (Okay, okay, I confess I have no willpower when it comes to cheese donuts!)

Next, at Tables for Tails, a popular café, I smelled a tangy blue cheese quiche. I bought a gigantic piece to serve for Aunt Sweetfur's birthday dinner.

Finally, in Singing Stone Square, I bought a beautiful flowering pink plant from Geraldine Greenwhiskers, the florist. Aunt Sweetfur loves flowers. It was the perfect gift!

Now, if only I could come up with the perfect idea for my book . . .

I'll Help You, Geronimo!

I got home just in time to greet my guests. The first to arrive was Grandfather William. He is a STICKLER for being on time. Then my sister, Thea, ROARED up on her motorcycle. Thea and I are opposites. She is a daredevil, and I am a scaredy-mouse! Next came my cousin Trap, who loves to tease me, followed by my dear nephew Benjamin.

While we waited for Aunt Sweetfur, we began to decorate the house with balloons and streamers.

Benjamin had made a purple banner (Aunt Sweetfur's favorite color) that read:

Thea Stilton

Aunt Sweetfur

HAPPY BIRTHDAY, AUNT SWEETFUR!

I grabbed a ladder so I could hang it over the fireplace. But as I climbed, the ladder began to **WOBBLE**.

"I'll help you, Germeister!" my cousin volunteered, **GRIPPING** the ladder.

I gulped. The last time Trap volunteered to help me, I ended up in the emergency room with a cheese grater stuck in my fur! But that's another story . . .

"Are you s-s-sure?" I stammered nervously.

"Don't you trust me?" Trap retorted.

Before I could answer, he began to sneeze . . .

"Ah-ah-ah . . . choo!"

As he leaned on the ladder, it fell, and I

TUMBLED to the ground, landing on my tail. Ouch!

Oh, when would I learn to trust my instincts and not my cousin?

"Are you okay, Uncle?" my nephew squeaked, running over.

I checked for broken bones. "I'm fine," I assured Benjamin, standing up.

Steady . . .

Don't worry!

Ah-ah-ah . . .

It was then, though, that I realized I had **broken** something . . . my watch!

Rats! I loved my WATCH! It was a gift from my grandfather when I took over *The Rodent's Gazette*.

Help!

. . . choo!

Tears **sprang** to my eyes, but Grandfather put a paw on my back and said, "Get a grip, Grandson. It's not the end of the world! I know how you can fix that watch. Bring it to my famouse watchmaker friend, Minute Mouse. You'll find him at his shop, **Time Flies!** He repairs and sells clocks. I think you'll find the place very **UNUSUAL** . . ."

Get a grip!

Sigh!

I was just about to ask him what he meant by **unusual** when the doorbell rang. Aunt Sweetfur had arrived!

"Happy birthday, Aunt Sweetfur!" we shouted.

The party was a big success! Aunt Sweetfur gave us all big **hugs** in appreciation. We had a fabumouse dinner (my quiche was a hit!) and delicious **strawberry cheesecake** for dessert. **Yum!**

TIME FLIES!

As soon as I left work the next day, I decided to go find **Time Flies!**, the clock shop Grandfather William had told me about.

I took the subway and got off in the western end of the city. From what Grandfather had told me, the shop was located on the **ALLEY OF LOST TIME**, in the oldest part of town.

I couldn't find the street listed on my map, so I hailed a taxi. But the **TAXI** didn't know the street, either. Eventually, I had him drop me off in **Remembrance Square**. I wandered along Memories Road, which led into Useless Regrets Avenue . . . until I realized I was completely *lost*!

I went into a **deli** to ask for directions, but the mouse behind the counter just blinked. "A clock shop on the Alley of Lost Time? Umm . . . it's this

Maybe that way . . .

Never heard of it!

way, or **MAYBE** that way . . ." he mumbled.

I continued on, asking everyone I passed for directions — mice on skateboards, **construction** mice, business mice — but everyone said the same thing: "Never heard of it!"

I was about to give up when I spotted an elderly lady. "**Time Flies!**?" she asked incredulously. "The clock shop on the Alley of Lost Time? Who gave you this address, young mouse?"

Oh yes!

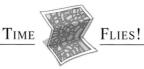

"My grandfather gave it to me," I explained.

"Your grandfather, eh? Now I understand. Once upon a time that shop was famouse, but almost no one remembers it anymore . . ." she said with a **FARAWAY** expression on her face. "No one remembers the corner cheese store where you could buy cheddar bread for a PENNY, or the candy store with the most delicious blue cheese **fudge** for a nickel . . ." She rambled on and on.

When she finally pointed me in the direction of the CLOCK SHOP, I thanked her for her help and continued on my way. After a few minutes, I saw the alley in front of me — but then a bus roared by, and when I looked up, the alley had DISAPPEARED! Huh? Were my eyes playing tricks on me? Was the cHeeSe falling off my cracker?

I shook my head, and the alley reappeared.

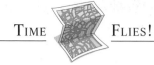

How strange!

I walked steadily ahead and soon found myself at the front door of the clock store. A huge antique WOODEN sign with a clock face on it hung over the doorway. It read: **Time Flies! Clock and Repair Shop.**

Underneath, in smaller writing, it read: Time waits for no mouse, so use your time wisely!

I went in, and it was then, right then, that this whole adventure truly began . . .

I'll Fix It!

As soon as I entered the dimly lit shop, I heard the steady rhythmic **TICKTOCK** of all the clocks surrounding me. There were big clocks, small clocks, and clocks in all different colors. There were ornate gold-plated clocks and wooden cuckoo clocks. There were chandelier clocks and clocks to sit on mantelpieces.

An instant later, I smelled the intense scent of **roses**. I followed the scent to a corner of the shop, where I discovered a huge blue pot filled with climbing roses. And when I say *climbing*, I mean, *climbing*! The flowered branches twisted together and went UP, **UP**, **UP**, all the way through a skylight in the roof.

That extraordinary plant grew half on the inside of the store and half on the outside.

I walked over to it and bent down to sniff the beautiful star-shaped flowers. Ah, there is nothing **sweeter** than the scent of fresh roses!

Suddenly, I felt a paw on my shoulder. "It's an amazing specimen, isn't it?" a voice squeaked in my ear. "This plant is called a Starry Rose. It holds a **MAGICAL SECRET** and comes from very, very far away . . ."

Sniff! Sniff!

Solution: The cuckoo clock on the left shows 3:30.

ALL THE CLOCKS SHOW THE SAME TIME... EXCEPT ONE. WHICH ONE?

I turned and saw a kindly-looking mouse about my grandfather's age. He had white hair and a **bushy** mustache, and he wore a pair of old-fashioned glasses. Right away, I knew this had to be **MINUTE MOUSE**, my grandfather's friend.

"Oh, hello. My grandfather, William Shortpaws, sent me. I have a watch in need of repair . . ." I began.

The old mouse brightened. "William? Of course, you must be his grandson Geronimo! I know all about you! William is so **PROUD** of you! He said that you are doing a great job running *The Rodent's Gazette* and that your books are fabumouse!"

"R-r-really?" I stammered.

I didn't say it aloud, but I was **shocked**! I mean, usually my grandfather likes to say things like, "Grandson, you need to work harder!" and "Grandson, you need to write **FASTER**!"

and "Grandson, the paper was so much better when I was publisher!"

I was still thinking about my grandfather when Minute Mouse yelled over his shoulder, "**Eloise**, look who came to visit us! William's grandson!"

From the back, an elderly rodent appeared. She had white hair and wore a dress **EMBROIDERED** with roses. "Oh, you really are the grandson of our dear friend William! I recognize you from the photo!" she exclaimed happily.

She showed me a photo of Grandfather and me in a **silver** frame. "Your grandfather gave me this," she explained. "He is so proud of you! He told us you were interviewed

on MouseTV and that you won the distinguished **Squeakiest Journalist** prize!"

Again, I was surprised. When my interview on MouseTV aired, Grandfather complained that it was on at the same time as **MONDAY NIGHT MOUSEBALL**. And when I won the Squeakiest Journalist prize, my grandfather snorted and said, "They're giving the prize to **YOU**?!"

Ah, well. Maybe one of these days I'd figure out Grandfather William. But for now I kissed the elderly lady's paw and said politely, "Pleased to meet you, ma'am!"

Pleased to meet you!

Oh!

She smiled. "What a *gentlemouse*, just like your grandfather! Now, please, make yourself comfortable!" she squeaked, leading me to a cozy room in the back of the store.

In addition to dozens of clocks on the walls, the room had a clock-faced rug and two pawchairs. Eloise motioned for me to sit in one of the chairs. It was **BLUE** with a yellow starry pattern. There were two enormouse **dragons** carved into the armrests, and a golden dragon head with **GLITTERING** eyes peered down from the backrest. I felt like I was sitting on some kind of throne! How strange!

I was about to ask Eloise what was with all the dragons, but right then Minute appeared. I showed him my **broken** watch, and he exclaimed, "Ah, I recognize this piece! I sold it to your grandfather many years ago. Don't worry, I'll fix it."

THERE'S NO TIME LIKE THE PRESENT!

Minute Mouse disappeared into his **workshop**, and I sank into the BLUe pawchair. Ah! It was so comfortable!

A moment later, Eloise returned with a cup of tea and a plate of **warm** cheesy cookies.

The teapot and sugar bowl were engraved with tiny clock designs, and the silver sugar spoon

was shaped like a clock hand. The cookies were shaped like numbers from ONE to TWELVE — just like (you guessed it!) the numbers on a clock. How coordinated!

I also noticed that even the napkins Eloise offered me had little sayings on them that were all about time. One read: There's no time like the present! Another read: Always make time for yourself!

Eloise sat in the pawchair across from me, working on a piece of embroidery (a clock design, of course!) and squeaking away.

"As you can see, we really like clocks. In fact, we hardly ever leave our shop, since our life revolves around everything within these walls," the elderly mouse revealed, looking around with a satisfied air.

"Every one of our clocks has a story," she continued. "For example, that one is an ancient

SUNDIAL that tells the time of day by the position of the sun. The sun hits the pointer, which casts a shadow on the stone tablet, marking the time. That one is a strange water clock, with a complicated system of gears and weights. And this is a RARE clock with detailed figures of a cat chasing a mouse."

I shivered. Who would want a clock with a cat chasing a mouse?

"This beautiful gold pocket watch belonged to the founder of New Mouse City, GRANT

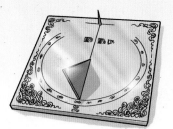

SUNDIAL

WATER CLOCK

GENTLEMOUSE. It sings the Mouse Island anthem every hour on the hour," Eloise went on. "But the piece that has the most value for Min is the watch that he made the very first day he began working with his grandfather, the great George Pawsley Clockers. It is the most valuable to him because it holds wonderful **memories**."

"That's nice," I mumbled, feeling a **wave** of sleepiness coming over me. I couldn't help it. That dragon pawchair was more comfortable than my super-deluxe, super-plush **SleepyRat**

CAT AND MOUSE CLOCK

POCKET WATCH

MattReSS! Before I could stop myself, I let out a loud yawn. Oh, how embarrassing!

"Excuse me," I apologized, turning **RED**.

"Don't worry, dear," Eloise said, with a kind smile. "That pawchair makes everyone sleepy. Min takes a nap there every day after lunch." Then she continued on with her story. "All these clocks were collected by the GRANDFATHER of the GRANDFATHER of the GRANDFATHER of my husband, and every one has a story. The most interesting story is about an ancient MAGICAL instrument kept in this store that is able to stop time and then make it go backward. It's called the Tick Tock Timepiece..."

I wanted to ask Eloise more about the Tick Tock Timepiece, but I felt another YAWN coming on and decided I'd better keep my mouth shut.

Still, I couldn't stop my eyelids from drooping. There was something about that pawchair and the

TICKTOCKING of the clocks that **relaxed** me. Before I knew it, I fell fast asleep and began to dream . . .
     and dream . . .
          and dream . . .

KNIGHT! KNIIIGHT! KNIIIIIIGHT!

I woke up because I thought I heard a **VOICE** calling.

"Iiight! Iiight!" the voice seemed to be saying. **HUH?**

I stood up and looked around. I was still in the clock shop, but it was **NIGHTTIME**. "Um, Mr. Minute Mouse, sir?" I called out tentatively. "Ms. Eloise?" But no one answered.

Just then the voice called out again. This time I realized what it was saying. **"Kniiiight! Kniiiight!"**

How very, very **STRANGE**. Even stranger, the voice was coming from the Starry Rose plant!

I ran to the plant and looked up at the skylight. The plant burst through the opening into a dark sky **sparkling** with stars.

It was then that I remembered how Minute Mouse had mentioned that the Starry Rose was a **magical** plant. Hmmm . . . Was the Starry Rose like the beanstalk in *Rat and the Beanstalk,* the old fairy tale I'd read when I was a young **MOUSELING**?

I was hoping Minute Mouse would appear to clear things up, but the voice began shrieking louder: "Kniiiight! Hello down there! What's taking you so long?!"

Of course, I had no idea what the voice was talking about, so I yelled back, "My name is *Stilton, Geronimo Stilton*. Who are you, and why are you **HOLLERING** up there?"

But the voice didn't answer my questions. In fact, it was sounding more and more exasperated by the minute. "Come on! I don't have all day, you know! Climb up! Climb up! Climb up! Let's get this show on the road!" it demanded.

I tried to ask another question, but the WIND took my voice away. Rats! If I wanted to know who was calling me, I had no choice. I had to climb up the plant. So I gave myself a **PEP TALK** and began climbing. Holey cheese, it was steep! Oh, why did I have to be afraid of heights?

I slipped and slid on the leaves, which were wet with dew, and the scent of the roses was so intense that it made my head SPIN. I love the sweet scent of flowers as much as the next mouse, but have you ever stuck your head in a rosebush for more than ten minutes? Let me tell you, it is pretty OVERPOWERING! In fact, it's almost suffocating! I was afraid that I would faint and go TUMBLING head over paws to the ground!

Headlines flashed before my eyes: *Sweet Scent Suffocates Stilton! Publisher Plunges from Monster Bush . . . Recovery Not So Rosy!*

As I climbed, I did my best not to look down. But you know how that goes . . . whenever someone tells you not to do something, you only want to do it more! Eventually, I snuck a peek. I was so HIGH up, I could see the entire city!

I climbed and climbed until I reached a sea of clouds as soft as my great-grandmother Fancyfur's wall-to-wall **cat fur** carpet. Come to think of it, everything in Great-Grandma Fancyfur's house was carpeted. Even her toilet seat!

Anyway, where was I? Oh yes, next I spotted a pink **shimmering** sky. It was then that I realized what was magical about the Starry Rose plant.

It led to the *Kingdom of Fantasy*!

In the
Kingdom
of
Fantasy

Crystal Castle!

Queen Blossom's Crystal Castle

THE KNIGHT OF THE SILVER WATER LILY

Closing my eyes, I jumped off the Starry Rose plant and landed safely in the white **blanket** of clouds. Whew!

I **polished** my glasses to see better, SQUiNTeD my eyes, and far, far, far into the horizon, I recognized the shining roof of Crystal Castle, the home of *Blossom*. Ah, Blossom, the Queen of the Fairies, Her Majestic Majesty, the Lady of Peace and Happiness, She Who Brings World Harmony, the Most Beautiful of Beauties. Dear, **sweet** Blossom had summoned me to her castle many times in the past few years. And now my adventures in the *Kingdom of Fantasy* were practically famouse!

I had met elves, ridden **UNICORNS**,

Blossom of the Flowers

NAME: Blossom of the Flowers; also called the White Queen, Lady of Peace and Happiness, She Who Brings World Harmony, Her Majestic Majesty, and the Most Beautiful of Beauties

WHO SHE IS: Queen of the fairies and the entire Kingdom of Fantasy

ORIGIN: She comes from the ancient and noble descendants of the Winged Ones.

RESIDENCE: Lives in the Kingdom of the Fairies, at Crystal Castle, a fantastic and magical castle made entirely of shiny, transparent crystal

SPECIAL ACCESSORIES: The blue rose is the symbol of Blossom of the Flowers. The queen always wears a blue rose ring, a blue rose necklace, and a crown of blue roses.

helped gnomes, fought **giants**, defeated trolls, destroyed witches, and saved princesses in the Kingdom of Fantasy. And every time was more **EXCITING** than the last!

I was still thinking about all my adventures when I heard the little voice again.

"**Kniiiiiiight!**"

I turned and saw in front of me a small creature dressed in a full suit of **shiny silver** armor, complete with a helmet, metal gloves, and leggings. In his hand he held a sword with a hilt in the shape of a water lily.

"Um, hello, small creature," I said. "What's your name?"

"Small creature?! It's me, Knight! Why are you calling me small creature? I mean, I am a small creature — but still, after all we've been through, how could you not **recognize** your old pal?" The small being huffed, clearly insulted.

I scratched my head. The voice did sound **familiar**, but why couldn't I place the face? Oh, right, it was completely covered by a helmet!

"Okay, Knight, I'll give you a hint," the small creature offered. "I am now a knight just like you. I am the **Knight of the Silver Water Lily**."

I thought hard. What kind of creature would like **WATER LILIES**?

Well, frogs, of course. Suddenly, I knew exactly who was behind that mask! It was my dear old **frog** friend **SCRIBBLEHOPPER**! He had been my guide on my first trip to the Kingdom of Fantasy and helped me on many of my other adventures to the kingdom after that.

"Scribblehopper, it's you!" I squeaked. I tried to give him a *hug*, but it was a little tricky with all that armor on.

"Check out my sword, Sir Geronimo!" Scribblehopper **croaked**. He waved it in the air, practically SLICING my whiskers off. "Oops!" he muttered. "The only problem with this armor is that it's so **HEAVY**. I can hardly take a step in it. By the way, can you please lift the visor of my helmet?"

I raised the VISOR, and the **NOSE** of my familiar friend appeared.

Here we go . . .

Thanks!

"Ah, finally, I can breathe!" the frog announced. Then he jumped out of the rest of the armor with a freeing **LEAP**. "Whew! It was like a sauna in there! I think I lost **ten pounds**!" he croaked.

Then his voiced **brightened**. "Well, now that I'm out, let's go see the queen!"

And just like that, we were off to find Queen Blossom!

The Kingdom of Fantasy

The Kingdom of Fantasy is endless because the imagination is endless! Anyone who can dream can explore it and discover even more new kingdoms within it.

Mysterious Abyss

Castle of Dreams

Kingdom of the Pixies

Land of Nightmares

Kingdom of the Fire Dragons

Kingdom of the Fairies

Land of Trolls

City of the Blue Unicorns

Kingdom of the Elves

Kingdom of the Witches

Land of Toys

Kingdom of the Diggerts

Land of Sweets

Land of the Ogres

Kneel Before the Queen! *Buuzzzz!*

We walked along the white CLOUDY trail for hours until we ended up in a green meadow filled with tons of COLORFUL flowers. The moon and the stars were disappearing, and soon the sun would come up, illuminating the Kingdom of the Fairies with rosy light. Oh, how I loved the Kingdom of the Fairies and its queen, *Blossom*.

However, right then I began to hear a strange sound . . .

Buuuuuuuzzzzzzzzzzzzzz!

And before I knew what was happening, Scribblehopper announced in a solemn tone, "Here you are . . . the queen!"

I looked around, but I didn't see CRYSTAL CASTLE, where Blossom lived. Instead I saw an enormouse tree with a gigantic **golden** beehive in it.

So that's where the buzzing was coming from!

A swarm of bees flew toward me, then formed an **arrow** that pointed at the beehive. "Hey, you! Buzz! Follow us, and no funny stuff, understand? The queen — buuzzzz — awaits you!" ordered the head of the swarm.

I blinked, then stammered, "Uh, the qu-qu-queen? What queen?"

I approached the beehive and saw a large bee standing on a minuscule balcony adorned with **PINK** flowers.

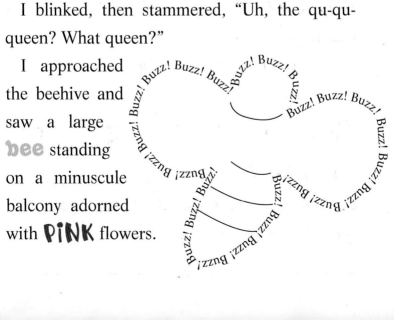

"Kneel before the queen! Buzz!" the head of the swarm commanded.

Then the head of the swarm STUNG me, just for good measure. OWWW! I gave a yelp, and hurried to kneel. I didn't want any more stings! Meanwhile, the queen looked down her nose at me and announced in a pompous tone, "Buuzzzz! Knight, I know all about you. And now — buuzzzz — my regal niece, the princess, is ready to leave. Buuuuzzzzzzzz!"

"Huh? Your niece? Leave for where?" I asked.

Scribblehopper hurried over, saying, "Don't worry, Your Majesty. The mouse — I mean, the knight — is a little SLOW on the uptake. But I'll handle him! So where is the little princess?"

Then he elbowed me and muttered, "Shhhh! We are already late, and I'll explain everything later, but here's the quick version: We need to save the *Kingdom of Fantasy*, and the little princess, niece of the queen of the bees, is coming with us!"

The head of the swarm proclaimed, "Little Princess Buzzy, niece of our beloved queen of the bees, the third of her name, of the noble Buzzers, is leaving the beehive on a grand ADVENTURE with *Sir Geronimo of Stilton* and with the Knight of the Silver Water Lily! All hail, Princess Buzzy!"

All the bees bowed in midair, buzzing, "Hail to Princess Buzzy! Buzz! Buzz! Buzzzzzz!"

LITTLE PRINCESS BUZZY

WHO SHE IS: Niece of the queen of the bees

ORIGIN: The noble Buzzers family

RESIDENCE: The Magic Golden Hive

SPECIAL ACCESSORY: The golden tiara she wears on her head

A second later, a little bee flitted toward us with her nose in the air, just like the queen. She was sprinkled with golden powder, and her wings shone with all the colors of the **RAINBOW**.

She was followed by a group of other little bees. Scribblehopper described each one to me in a low voice. "That's the hairdresser for the little princess . . . the **massage therapist** for the little princess . . . the MAKEUP ARTIST for the little princess . . . the WING POLISHER for the little princess . . . the SEAMSTRESS for the little princess . . . the personal trainer for the little princess . . . the ACTIVITIES COORDINATOR for the little princess . . . the public relations consultant for the little princess . . .

RUBSY,
THE MASSAGE THERAPIST

CLIPSY,
THE HAIRDRESSER

HEMSY,
THE SEAMSTRESS

My jaw dropped. "Do we have to bring **all** of them with us?" I whispered to Scribblehopper.

Unfortunately, the little princess heard me and began to HUFF. "*Buuzzzz!* How dare you! I am of ROYAL BLOOD! Do I have to sting you in the snout so you don't forget?!"

She launched herself toward me, but her life skills coach stopped her. "Think before you sting, Little Princess! Will stinging solve your problem?" she cautioned.

"Will stinging solve *your* problem?" the little princess muttered under her breath in a

Wait for me!

singsongy voice. One thing was clear about Princess Buzzy: She didn't like being told what to do!

After the princess put away her stinger, Scribblehopper announced, "We're off to see the QUEEN!"

Finally! I couldn't wait to see Queen Blossom! Scribblehopper led the way, with the bees following close behind. I went last, squeaking, "Wait for me!"

Follow me!

I Am Queen of the Greenbloods!

This time, Scribblehopper led us into a forest. We followed a GRAVEL trail that wound through raspberry and blueberry bushes until it stopped in front of a pond where pink WATER LILIES floated. The pond was near a waterfall, and next to it was a rock in the shape of a heart. A well-dressed toad perched on the rock.

Strangely, the toad looked like Scribblehopper.

"There she is!" croaked my frog friend, waving his WEBBED hand.

"Wait a minute," I interrupted. "I thought we were going to see the queen!"

"She is a queen — and she's my toad cousin. Queenie, over here!" Scribblehopper called.

HOW MANY WATER LILY FLOWERS ARE IN THE POND?

Hey! Queenie!

It seemed Queenie was the sister of the niece of the aunt of the grandmother of the great-grandmother of **SCRIBBLEHOPPER'S** mother.

Queenie looked at me with a **snooty** expression. "And who might you be, Mouse? Do you have a title? Are you at least a **count** or a *prince* or something?" she croaked haughtily.

"Ahem, no, I am only a **knight**," I admitted. "But that's enough for me, to tell you the truth."

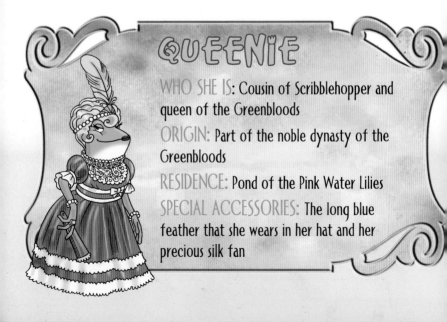

QUEENIE

WHO SHE IS: Cousin of Scribblehopper and queen of the Greenbloods

ORIGIN: Part of the noble dynasty of the Greenbloods

RESIDENCE: Pond of the Pink Water Lilies

SPECIAL ACCESSORIES: The long blue feather that she wears in her hat and her precious silk fan

Queenie sniffed as if she **smelled** something unpleasant. "Well, I am of royal blood. I am part of the noble dynasty of the Greenbloods," she informed me with a wave of her silk fan.

Scribblehopper hurried to introduce me. "Queenie, this is Sir Geronimo of Stilton. He doesn't look like much and he's kind of a **klutz**, but we're all going to see the queen together."

Thankfully, this time we headed off in the direction of Blossom's CRYSTAL CASTLE.

NOT LOOKING GOOD

At last we arrived at Blossom's castle, crossing through the pure crystal entrance and down the **long** corridor filled with tall shiny columns. When we reached the glittering Throne Room where the Queen of the Fairies receives her guests, I looked around.

STRANGE . . . there was no one sitting on the throne.

And in the distance, I saw a group of fairies with SAD expressions.

The fairies surrounded a very elderly fairy who leaned on a crystal cane with a DIAMOND knob.

Maybe the old fairy knows where to find Queen Blossom, I thought. Isn't there some saying about our elders being a treasure trove of hidden knowledge? I strode up to the old fairy and said, "Excuse me, could you tell me where I might find the very **beautiful** and beloved Queen of the Fairies, Blossom?"

The ancient one lifted her veil, revealing white hair, **deep** wrinkles, and a tired expression.

Behind me Scribblehopper croaked, "Oh no!"

The little princess buzzed, "Holey honeycombs!"

And Queenie muttered, "Not looking good."

I had no idea what they were talking about until the old fairy said in a weak voice, "Knight, I recognize you, but alas, you don't recognize me. I am Blossom, Queen of the Fairies."

Only then did I realize that the

fairy wore a *blue rose* ring on her finger, just like Blossom! And around her neck she wore a *blue rose* medallion, and on her head was a *blue rose* crown!

But above all, I noticed the fairy's eyes, as **BLUE** as the spring sky.

"Forgive me, Majesty. I did not recognize you," I said.

"It's all right, Knight," Blossom answered kindly. "I hardly **recognize** myself!"

CHEESY PIES AND FLY SOUFFLÉ

"How can we help?" I wailed, starting to sob uncontrollably. Then Scribblehopper began crying, followed by Princess Buzzy. Finally, even snooty Queenie BROKE DOWN. Yep, it was a regular cry-fest. In fact, we cried so much, our tears formed a lake on the crystal floor. I made a mental note to watch my step. Tears on a crystal surface could make things pretty SLIPPERY.

Blossom waved her hand to get our attention and said, "Friends, remember that for every problem, there is a solution! It's just waiting to be found."

She smiled and continued, "Now let's forget about this sadness for a while. I'm sure you are all **HUNGRY** after your long journey. So I suggest we sit down together and share a wonderful meal." She clapped her hands. "Fairy of the Kitchen, can you prepare our dinner?"

A smiling fairy flew toward us, wearing a white apron, a cap, and little **round** glasses. "Of course, Your Highness," sang the fairy, whose

name was Simmereen. She pointed us toward a **LONG** banquet table.

The table had a blue silk tablecloth and was set with the finest china. The glasses were made of PURE CRYSTAL and were engraved with roses. Whenever they were touched, they made a **sweet** sound.

Yes, that table was certainly set for a very *fancy* feast. There was only one thing missing: the meal!

Right then my stomach began to **gurgle**. Oh, how embarrassing!

"Um, Simmereen," Scribblehopper asked. "Do you have any **food** to go along with those plates?"

The fairy bent over, laughing.

"Never fear, Frog," she said. "Food is on its way."

Then she began to **sing**.

"Cheesy pies and fly soufflé,
nectar rolls made fresh today!
Lots of treats for all to eat;
take a plate, then have a seat!
With my wand I stir the air,
and make a meal beyond compare!"

Like **magic**, a delicious-looking meal appeared before our very eyes.

For every guest, the fairy had conjured up an appropriate dish. There was a giant green leaf **BRIMMING** with all kinds of flowers for Little Princess Buzzy, candied larva bites for Scribblehopper, and a fly pie with a side of **gnat sauce** for Queenie. For me, there was enough cheese to make a grown mouse cry tears of joy!

Here you go!
Bon appétit!

We all attacked our meals like we were STARVING prisoners. And when we were finished, Scribblehopper let out a loud **burp**! So much for table manners . . .

FRESH FLOWERS FOR PRINCESS BUZZY

CANDIED LARVA BITES FOR SCRIBBLEHOPPER

FLY PIE WITH GNAT SAUCE FOR QUEENIE

MIXED CHEESES FOR SIR GERONIMO

THIS IS SOLITAIRE

After we ate, we gathered in front of *Queen Blossom*.

She led us to a wall of the Throne Room where there was an engraved CRYSTAL plaque. Its message was written in the Fantasian alphabet.* Can you translate it?

⊄⊀♪ ⊽⊀⌐◻⊀⊄ ⏀⟡⟊⊽
⊗Υ ⊄⊀♪ ⟒⊥⊿⊖⊵⧨
⊗Υ Υ⟡⊿⊄⟡⊽⊷

---

* You can find the Fantasian alphabet on page 310.

THE SECRET LAWS OF THE KINGDOM OF FANTASY

1. The Kingdom of Fantasy is protected by the Queen of the Fairies, Blossom of the Flowers.

2. The Kingdom of Fantasy is as infinite as Queen Blossom's capacity to dream.

3. If the life of the queen comes to an end, the entire kingdom perishes with her.

4. The life of Queen Blossom is measured by the enchanted clock that is found in the Land of Time.

It said: THE SECRET LAWS OF THE KINGDOM OF FANTASY. We read through them.

"I'm sure you are wondering why I look so **old**," Blossom began. "**TIME**, for me, has begun passing more *quickly* than the north wind. And, unfortunately, time is also passing at an increased rate for **everyone** I protect. If we do not fix time, I will **perish** — and so will the entire Kingdom of Fantasy!"

Blossom looked into her silver and ruby mirror. She said, "According to the kingdom's secret laws, the enchanted clock held in the Land of Time is broken — that is why I am getting older every second! If I die, the entire *Kingdom of Fantasy* will no longer **exist**!"

Her eyes filled with tears.

"I implore you, Knight, to travel to the mysterious Land of Time, find TICK TOCK,

the Wizard of Time, and ask him to repair the enchanted clock. For centuries, we've kept **perfect** time. I am worried that something has happened to **Tick Tock**!"

I **CHEWED** my whiskers. What if something *had* happened to Tick Tock? Something **BAD**? Oh, why were these adventures always so scary?! Why couldn't they take place in a relaxing **seaside resort** or in the quiet, peaceful countryside? But the queen needed my help, so before I could change my mind, I squeaked, "I'll **do it!**"

After I agreed, the queen ordered her maids to bring me my **ARMOR** and a special bag for the trip.

I slipped into the armor. Then I checked myself out in the mirror. I'm not one to brag, but I thought I

looked pretty **FIERCE** for a
scaredy-mouse!

The fairies also brought me a
beautiful **RED** velvet satchel.

"Knight, this is a **magical bag**," Blossom
explained. "It will shrink or expand in size when
you require it. Inside, you will find
everything you need for your journey,
including a **feather pen** so you can write
about your adventures."

Not long after that, a fantastic carriage pulled
up in front of the castle. It was shaped like a shell
and drawn by a thousand **pink** butterflies!

"With this **MAGIC** carriage, you will travel to
the mysterious Land of Time," said the queen.

Everything was ready for our departure, but
right then Scribblehopper cleared his throat and
croaked, "Ahem, Your Majesty, how do
we reach the mysterious **Land of Time**?

It's so mysterious that even I, one of the most expert guides, don't know how to get there."

"Never fear, dear frog — I've thought of that," Blossom replied, clapping her hands. "Meet your guide to the Land of Time!"

A mysterious **tall** and slender warrior arrived. He wore silver armor and carried a sword.

I was dying to know who was clanking around inside that suit of armor, but with the face mask down, I couldn't **SEE** a thing.

"This is **Solitaire**, the Lone Knight," Blossom announced, waving the knight forward. "You may call him by name, but please be advised that he will not respond to you, because he has made a *vow of silence*."

Then she turned to the knight. "Dear Knight, from now on you will be part of this BAND OF TIME SEEKERS. Please take them to the mysterious Land of Time."

Solitaire bowed to the queen, then turned and stared at us. Well, I guessed he was staring at us, but I couldn't be sure, because of the mask. There was a LONG pause, and I thought the knight was about to say something. I was wrong. He just *pointed* to the door and motioned for us to follow him.

To be honest, the whole not-talking thing was kind of CREEPY, but who am I to question a member of the queen's staff? Maybe it would be a nice change from Scribblehopper's chatter!

Outside, the knight CLIMBED into the golden shell carriage, and we clambered in next to him.

A moment later, the butterflies flapped their wings, lifting us UP, UP, UP into the air and off on another extraordinary adventure in the Kingdom of Fantasy . . .

Good luck!

Forget It,
Frog Breath!

We traveled for about seventy million billion hours toward the mysterious Land of Time. (Okay, it wasn't really seventy million billion hours, but it sure felt like it!) Princess Buzzy and Queenie were arguing the whole time.

"I must be the first to enter the Land of Time," insisted Queenie. "It's only right, since I am the only QUEEN on this trip. I am queen of the noble dynasty of the Greenbloods!"

"Forget it, Frog Breath!" Little Princess Buzzy countered. "I am the only *royal* one here. I am Princess Buzzy of the bees! Green blood? Yuck! Don't make me sick!"

The morning turned into afternoon, which

turned into night. But those two just wouldn't stop **bickering**.

I tried everything to block them out.

1 First I put on **PADDED earmuffs**, but they were so tight my ears turned red. Ow!

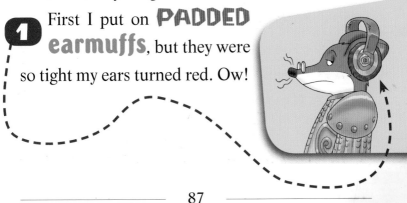

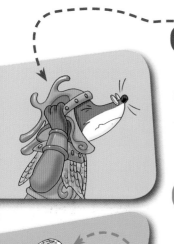

2 Then I tried to cover my ears with my **knight's helmet**. But I could still hear.

3 Finally, I tried wrapping my ears in a pair of clean **UNDERPANTS** from the bag Blossom had given me. But that didn't work, either. Rats!

For a minute I thought Scribblehopper had managed to distract them by telling stories about the Land of Time. "It's not like any other land. It guards the greatest treasure . . ." he began.

Unfortunately, as soon as the two heard the word treasure, they both began to

scream even louder.

"A treasure? What kind of treasure? Gold? Pearls? Precious jewels? Oh, if there are **EMERALDS**, I must have them!" Queenie shrieked. "Emeralds are **green**, of course, just like the color of my **aristocratic** blood. I'm not sure if I mentioned it yet, but I am of the highest royalty, you know — a descendant of the dynasty of the Greenbloods."

Princess Buzzy rolled her eyes. "If I hear the word *Greenbloods* one more time I will scream! Who cares about your ridiculous dynasty? Do you have any idea how *noble* we Buzzing Bees are? If there is a treasure, the most precious jewels belong to me!"

At this, Queenie flew into a rage. "How dare you attack my forefroggers!" she croaked. Then she reached over to **SWAT** the little princess like, well, like a bug. I didn't want the bee to get squashed, so I jumped in front of her and got swatted instead. Ouch!

Scribblehopper sighed. "Do you see, Knight?" he muttered sadly. "This is what always happens when you speak of the Land of Time and its **LEGENDARY TREASURE**. It triggers the curiosity and GREED of many . . ."

And so, with the queen and the little princess still squabbling, and with Scribblehopper chattering away in my ear, we continued on our way. Eventually, we reached the mysterious *Trail of the Seven Steps*, where we would find the mysterious *Door of Courage*, which would bring us to the even more mysterious Land of Time!

YOU MUST WALK BACKWARD!

At **dawn**, the shell carriage landed softly in a grassy field. The butterflies were **exhausted**. They sucked up a little **NECTAR** from some flowers and instantly fell asleep. We crept away on tiptoe, following Solitaire to a **LARGE** rock in the shape of a pyramid. A **MYSTERIOUS** message was carved on the rock in the Fantasian alphabet.* Can you read it?

* You can find the Fantasian alphabet on page 310.

1. ONLY TWO TRAVELERS A DAY MAY PASS!

2. WAIT UNTIL THE SUN RISES IN THE MORNING.

3. BLINDFOLD YOURSELF.

4. WALK BACKWARD.

5. COUNT SEVEN STEPS.

6. PASS THROUGH THE DOOR OF COURAGE . . . AND YOU WILL REACH THE LAND OF TIME!

TRAIL OF SEVEN STEPS

It said: *Door of Courage*. And just above it, a long list of instructions for entering the Land of Time was **engraved**:

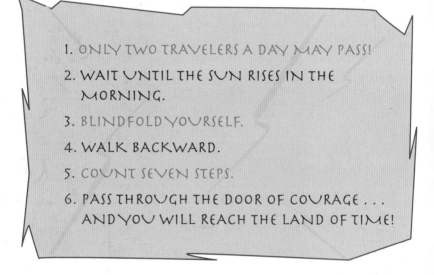

1. ONLY TWO TRAVELERS A DAY MAY PASS!
2. WAIT UNTIL THE SUN RISES IN THE MORNING.
3. BLINDFOLD YOURSELF.
4. WALK BACKWARD.
5. COUNT SEVEN STEPS.
6. PASS THROUGH THE DOOR OF COURAGE . . . AND YOU WILL REACH THE LAND OF TIME!

This was it. I shivered. The path to take was right there — the Trail of Seven Steps . . .

Scribblehopper coughed, trembling. "Ahem, I think you need c-c-courage to pass through the *Door of Courage*. And it looks like only two of us can pass through. Who do you think should go?" he said.

Believe me, I didn't want to go, but what could I do? I had told *Blossom* I would help. So I made a quick decision. "Scribblehopper, you, Princess Buzzy, and Queenie will return to Blossom with the *magic carriage*. Solitaire and I will continue on to the Land of Time," I squeaked, trying not to notice Scribblehopper doing a little *happy* dance.

"What's so **scary** about this place, anyway?" I asked the frog.

Everyone knows about the door!

"Oh, Knight, you are so naïve," Scribblehopper replied. "Everyone knows about the *Door of Courage*. Many have passed through, but no one has ever returned!"

I *twisted* my tail. Oh, why do

these adventures have to start in such terrifying ways? Just once it would be nice if someone met us at the door to a new land with a smile, a HUG, and maybe a platter of **chocolate Cheesy Chews**.

"Actually, the one who knows the most about this land is Blossom's brother, Prince Lucky," the frog explained. "Too bad no one knows where he is. According to the mysterious PROPHECY OF A THOUSAND HEARTS, one day Prince Lucky, along with a mysterious creature with one pen, four eyes, **one hundred** brains, and one thousand hearts will save Blossom."

"A creature with a pen, four eyes, one hundred brains, and a thousand hearts? But **who** could that be?" I muttered.

"Who knows?" said Scribblehopper. "That's why it's called a MYSTERIOUS prophecy. Do I have to **explain** everything?"

I blinked. By now, my fur was **STANDING** on end. I definitely could have done without the part about no one ever returning from the *Door of Courage*, but I couldn't let Blossom down.

The sun had fully risen, and Scribblehopper gave Solitaire two **BLINDFOLDS**. The knight handed one to me and covered his eyes. Before I could even squeak, Solitaire started walking backward . . . and DISAPPEARED.

Um . . . I'm coming . . .

"Um . . . I'm coming . . ." I said. With **trembling** paws, I covered my eyes with the blindfold and proceeded to walk backward, which wasn't easy. Did I mention I'm not the most **COORDINATED** mouse? I have trouble drinking my tall nonfat cheesy latte (hold the whipped cream) and reading the paper at the same time!

As I walked, I started counting my steps out loud. "ONE . . . TWO . . . THREE . . . FOUR . . . FIVE . . . SIX . . ."

When I reached six steps, my body **froze**. Only one more step, and I'd pass through the Door of Courage. Unfortunately, whatever courage I had mustered had **vanished**!

"I c-c-can't do this . . ." I stammered, reaching for my blindfold. Just then I heard Scribblehopper croaking, "Look, Knight! There's a giant piece of **FLYING CHEESE** right behind you!"

Flying cheese?

"Flying cheese?!" This I had to see. I was just about to take off my blindfold as I took **one more step** backward. Ack! To my horror, I had stepped straight off the edge of a cliff! I fell down, down, down . . .

While I **fell**, I heard Scribblehopper's croak echoing: "**SSOOOOOORRY**, Knight! . . . It seeeemed like yooou . . . neeeeeded a little heeeeeelp . . . reaching the *Door of Courage!*"

Ahhhh!

99

IF YOUR HEART
IS PURE . . .

As I fell toward the Door of Courage, I found myself surrounded by fine GOLDEN SAND. How strange! The sand **DRAGGED** me down like the powerful current of a river. But where was it taking me?

Suddenly, I heard a song:

"If your heart is filled with love,
and is kind, gentle, and pure,
you may reach the Land of Time;
of this you can be sure!
But if your heart is filled with greed,
and is uncaring and cold,
you will remain here forever,
growing bitter, gray, and old!"

Only then did I understand that the *Door of Courage* was in the shape of an immense golden hourglass! The sand was dragging me toward the center of the hourglass. I started to see other shapes around me. I soon figured out that the shapes were travelers who had tried to pass through the *Door of Courage* to go to the Land of Time . . . but who were trapped in the hourglass forever because their hearts were filled with greed! Rancid rat hairs! Would I remain trapped there forever, too?

Right then I reached the narrowest point of the hourglass.

I tried to concentrate. There was only one reason why I wanted to go to the Land of Time.

An **HOURGLASS** is an instrument that measures the passage of time. It is formed by two transparent bulbs united and connected to each other by a small hole. It can contain water, sand, or other similar substances. When an hourglass is turned over, the substance inside drains from one bulb into the other, always taking the same amount of time to empty completely.

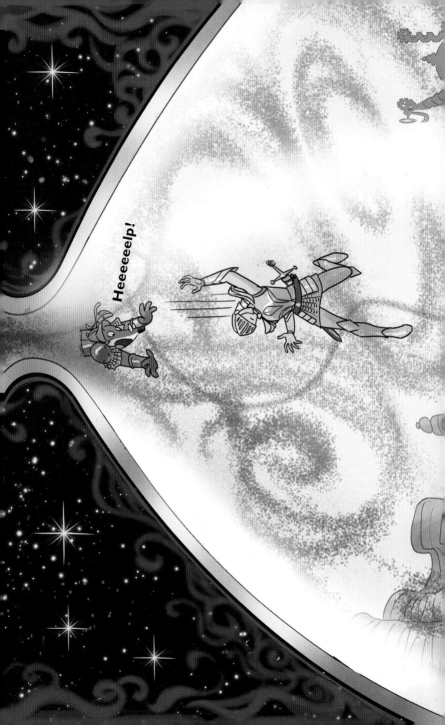

I wasn't looking for money or jewels. I just wanted to **save** Queen Blossom.

Concentrating on that thought of pure love, I TUMBLED through the center of the hourglass and slipped out the other side. **I made it!** I fell down, down, down until I hit the bottom of the glass.

Next thing I knew, the hourglass magically disappeared, and I found myself in the Land of Time . . .

THE LAND OF TIME

1. Desert of Memories
2. Plains of Punctuality — shaped like a clock
3. Castle of Time — resembles an antique alarm clock
4. Hill of the Dawn Alarm — has a tree in the shape of a rooster
5. River of Latecomers — where the water flows in reverse
6. Mount Minute — has a rock in the shape of an hourglass

The Land of Time

IN THE DESERT OF MEMORIES

The first thing I noticed was that I had landed in a SANDY desert. The next thing I noticed was that there was a terrific WIND and I was getting pelted by a million grains of pure gold powder. It stung my eyes and coated my fur, making it hard to walk. Oh, where was a nice outdoor shower when you needed one?

Fortunately, at that moment, a strong hand grabbed me by the paw and pulled me behind a BIG ROCK. It was Solitaire! I was so glad to see him I started SQUEAKING happily. He just nodded and wrote these words in the sand: Let's go. Blossom cannot wait.

My happiness quickly FADED as I thought

about *Blossom* getting older so quickly. Solitaire set out with decisive steps, nodding for me to follow.

He seemed to know the path well. HOW STRANGE!

We marched in that golden desert for hours and hours. I got more and more tired, and **blisters** formed on my paws. I thought about stopping to see if Blossom had packed any *bandages* in the magic bag, but I didn't want to seem like a wimp, so I kept going.

As we crunched along, Solitaire wrote another message in the sand. It read: This is the Desert of Memories.

Huh. I wondered how he knew that. I was too **tired** to find out. The only thing I would remember about this desert was that I never wanted to come back to it!

Finally, we saw the silhouette of a castle on the

horizon. It glittered in the sunlight because it was made entirely of gold!

We approached it in silence. Well, Solitaire was silent because of his silent-vow thing, but I was so blown away by the sight of the sparkling castle I couldn't speak. What a magnificent SHIMMERING construction!

Above the door, there was an enormouse clock. On each side of the door, there was a statue — one of a prince holding a **SWORD** and one of a queen holding a **rose**. Was it my imagination, or did the queen look just like Queen Blossom?

The face of the clock showed the **moon** and the **SUN**, and the hours were marked by precious stones.

But the strangest thing was that the hands of the clock were turning very quickly!

Near the clock there was a golden plaque. I read it aloud.

In the Kingdom of Fantasy, I am the heart.

I signal the hours, the stop, and the start.

I signal the life of Blossom the queen,

our wonderful ruler, so kind and serene.

But if I am crossed, then the hours will fly,

and Blossom will grow old, wither, and die.

The Wizard of Time can fix me, it's true,

for he is the genius who made me brand-new.

Under the plaque, words were **engraved** in the Fantasian alphabet.* Can you translate them?

⤙⊤⌐⌐🔊 ⤙⊙⌐⌐🔊
⤙⊤⊓♪⌐⊤♪⌐⌐ ♪

* You can find the Fantasian alphabet on page 310.

The Fantasian writing said Tick Tock Timepiece.
This was it!

Then I noticed that on the clock face there was
a signature:

Constructed by Tick Tock, the Wizard of Time,
King of Mechanisms,
Prince of the Gears,
Emperor of Contraptions

I also noticed that the hands were being
pushed by the wind **SWEEPING** through the
DESERT OF MEMORIES.

Suddenly, someone tapped my back. I nearly
JUMPED out of my fur! Was it a witch,
a wizard, or a terrifying playful kitten?
Lucky for me, it was only Solitaire. He was so
quiet I forgot he was there!

The knight motioned for me to **climb** onto
his shoulders so I could reach the clock face. We

had to try to fix the clock! I tried to **STOP** the hands, or at least to **SLOW** them down, but they were moving too fast.

Next, **Solitaire** passed me his sword to see if I could cut the hands off the clock. But the metal was too hard to sever, and instead I nearly **CHOPPED** my tail in two! Rats!

There wasn't anything we could do. That **SINISTER** wind was too strong to stop.

THE LABYRINTH
OF ILLUSIONS

Solitaire helped me down from the clock. Thank goodmouse! I was getting *dizzy* up there!

At that point, there was only one way to stop the **TICK TOCK TIMEPIECE**. We had to enter the castle and find the **Wizard of Time**. Since he invented the clock, he would certainly know how to repair it, right?

Too bad the castle was built like a **SAFE**!

I tried pushing open the front door and hurt my shoulder. Then I tried *knocking* and nearly broke every bone in my paw! **YOUCH**!

Meanwhile, Solitaire appeared to be waiting for something to happen. **Strange!**

Soon the hands of the clock *whirled* around and hit twelve o'clock. Suddenly, the two statues next to the clock came to life! The prince statue **STRUCK** the gong with his sword, and a deep sound rang out.

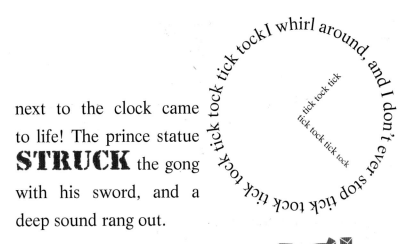

tick tock tick tock tick tock I whirl around, and I don't ever stop tick tock tick tock tick tock

tick tock tick tick tock tick tock

GONNNNG!

The queen statue held out her flower, and sweet **music** filled the air all around us.

Then the giant doors of the Castle of Time slowly opened for us!

Deep inside the CASTLE we glimpsed a sparkling light . . .

I ran toward the light, but I hit a wall and BOUNCED off it like a rubber ball.

BOING!

Only then did I understand that I had bumped

into an enormouse crystal hourglass. I went past it and found myself in front of thousands of **small** and **LARGE** gears that formed a twisting maze.

Cheese and crackers!

How would I find the right path to make it through the maze?

EENY, MEENY, MINEY, MO . . .

I stared at the paths, bewildered. Which one should I choose? There was only one way to decide. I pointed to each path while squeaking, "Eeny, meeny, miney, mo . . ." Before I could continue, though, Solitaire cleared his throat. I gasped. Was the knight going to speak?! No such luck. Instead, Solitaire gestured for me to follow him. Then he began walking CONFIDENTLY, turning to the LEFT, to the RIGHT, to the LEFT, to the LEFT, to the RIGHT, to the LEFT . . .

I was glad Solitaire seemed to know where he was going, because I was completely lost!

Finally, after one last turn, we ended up in a golden hall. Its high ceilings were painted with glittering stars.

In the center of the room, I saw an old man with **snow-white** hair, and a full beard and mustache. He wore a blue robe embroidered with stars and planets. On his head he had a POINTY hat, and on his feet he wore slippers with curled toes.

He was sitting on a **gold** throne decorated with a sun and a moon.

This had to be Tick Tock, the **Wizard of Time**!

He gazed at us with a *penetrating* stare. It made me nervous.

"H-hello, my name is Stilton, Geronimo Stilton, and this is, um, **SILENCE** — I mean, Soundless — I-I mean, **Solitaire**," I mumbled.

The wizard didn't blink. I wondered if he ever lost a **staring contest**. I was about to ask him when I heard a noise. It sounded like

someone clearing their throat.

The throat clearing was followed by a **COUGH**, then a snort, some cracking of knuckles, and a little whistling. Finally, a **DEEP** voice next to me announced, "Hello, Father. It's me."

I turned in **SHOCK**. Solitaire, the silent knight, was speaking!

Solitaire **slowly** lifted his helmet, and I saw

Solitaire the Knight, also known as Prince Lucky

Lucky is the son of the Wizard of Time and brother of Blossom, Queen of the Fairies. He is one of the very noble descendants of the Winged Dynasty. A long time ago, when he left the Land of Time, he made a pledge of silence and promised to only speak again when he saw his father.

that his eyes were the same deep blue as the eyes of the Wizard of Time. Strangely, they also were the same color as Queen Blossom's eyes!

Now I was completely confused. **WHO** was Solitaire? Why did he call the wizard *Father*? And what was the deal with the **BLUE EYES**?

Solitaire set the record straight. "I am **Prince Lucky**, son of the Wizard of Time and Blossom's brother. This is the Room of Secrets, where the Secret of Time is held. It has been **SAFEGUARDED** for centuries by my beloved father. He is the inventor of the enchanted clock," he explained.

PEACLOCK THE
PEACOCK

Solitaire, or rather Prince Lucky, approached the wizard and said in a grave tone, "Father, we need your help. *Blossom* — your daughter, my sister — is in trouble. Now that the Tick Tock Timepiece is broken, she's getting older faster than ever. You've got to fix that clock, or the Kingdom of Fantasy will **DIE** with her!"

But the wizard just stared at him with an *odd* look on his face, and said, "Young Knight, I have no idea who you are. And I have no idea what you are JABBERING about."

The prince turned PALE. Clearly this wasn't the heartwarming father–son reunion he had always dreamed about!

Just then an enormouse peacock flew into the room. It had a shiny golden body and incredible sapphire-blue feathers. The bird landed silently near the wizard's throne and proudly opened its long tail. Amazing! At the ends of the peacock's feathers were tiny little golden clocks!

The peacock bowed to Prince Lucky, and said, "Oh, my dear Prince Lucky, my name is Peaclock. I am the trusted advisor to the Wizard of Time, and I'm afraid I have some terribly sad news for you. Your father has lost his memory and doesn't recognize anything or anyone!"

Prince Lucky looked crushed but urged the bird to continue. And so he did. "It all began here, in the Desert of Memories. An **EVIL** wind began to blow — the Wind of the West that comes from the KINGDOM OF THE WITCHES. Every day, it gets a little stronger."

As he spoke, we heard the wind howl. He continued. "You see, the Tick Tock Timepiece, which controls the life of Blossom and the entire duration of the Kingdom of Fantasy, is not **broken**. It works perfectly well, just like when your father first made it. The truth is that the strong and evil *WINDS OF THE WEST* are pushing the hands of the clock faster and faster!"

Peaclock stopped to wipe a **tear** from his eye with one long feather. Then he added bitterly, "I know who started that wind. It was the **WICKED WITCH ECLIPSE**, the same evil creature who sometimes provokes the salty Rain of Sadness."

As soon as the bird mentioned the **RAIN OF SADNESS**, a sudden rainstorm erupted.

Peaclock rolled his eyes and muttered, "See? She heard me speak of her **wickedness** and wanted to prove it. What a show-off." He **LOWERED** his voice and continued, "Still, you should know that the witch's powers are becoming increasingly powerful. She has strong alliances with many **CREATURES OF THE DARK SIDE**, including the Orcs of Bad Teeth, the Thieving Owls, the Red Scorpions, the Bottom Biters, the Lunar Werewolves, and others!"

I shivered. Oh, why couldn't the witch become friends with some creatures of the bright side? Couldn't she find some *Cheery Chimpanzees* or Kindly Kingfish or something?

I was still thinking about the witch's friends when Prince Lucky said, "Knight, you must go to the Kingdom of the Witches and bring to an end the Wind of the West!"

"**M-m-me?**" I gulped. "But what about you? Couldn't you come with me? Or maybe you could even go without me. I'm feeling a little **sick**," I squeaked, pretending to cough.

Lucky explained that he needed to stay and take care of his father.

MOLDY MOZZARELLA! My heart hammered as I chewed my pawnails like they were my last meal.

"You can do it, Knight," the prince said. "Remember the mysterious **PROPHECY OF A THOUSAND HEARTS**, which says that Prince Lucky may save the Kingdom of Fantasy thanks to a creature with one pen, four eyes, one hundred brains, and one thousand hearts?"

"Yeeesss . . ." I said. But what was his point?

"Don't you understand, Knight? The prophecy is about you! You have a PEN because you are a writer! You have FOUR EYES because you wear glasses! You have ONE HUNDRED BRAINS because you are smart! And most important, you have one thousand hearts because you are generous and kind! This is why Blossom chose YOU to help save the Kingdom of Fantasy!" explained the prince.

I couldn't believe it. The prophecy *was* about me! I wasn't sure about the hundred brains or the tHouSanD HeaRtS bits, but it was clear that Blossom needed me. I couldn't let her down.

TA-DA!

Prince Lucky assured me that I would not be **ALONE** on my journey to the Kingdom of the Witches. "You will have a trusty guide and detailed directions to get you to the Tower of Fear, where **ECLIPSE** lives," he said. "But before you leave, we must have a going-away party!" he announced.

He took me to the balcony to see the large crowd gathered below.

Millisecond Sprites

Minute Gnomes

I saw Millisecond Sprites, **SMALL** and jumpy. Then there were Minute Gnomes, who specialized in alarm clocks. Their leader, Sixty Seconds, offered me a shiny gold alarm clock.

"A **TRAVELER** without an alarm clock is like a . . . like a . . . well, a traveler without an alarm clock!" he declared. Sixty might not have been filled with words of WISDOM, but I could tell he meant well.

Next I saw dancing Hour Fairies and bearded Century Elves. There was also a giant named Eon,

Hour Fairies

Century Elves

the oldest inhabitant in all of the Land of Time. Eon was the only one in the entire kingdom who was old enough to remember every **ancient legend** ever written. Now, that's pretty old!

A loud cheer erupted from the crowd. "Hooray for the knight! Hooray for Sir Geronimo of Stilton! Best wishes to the knight who is about to go to the TERRIFYING and dangerous Kingdom of the Witches to fight the wicked witch ECLIPSE! Good luck to the knight, who may never return, or if he does — which is highly unlikely — may not return in one piece! At the very least he will lose his tail!"

I gulped. The crowd stared up at me expectantly. I knew I should give an inspiring speech, but all I could stammer was, "Th-thanks. I'll t-t-try my b-b-best."

After that I was served a DELICIOUS meal in the banquet hall.

Here is the menu:

Appetizers

Assorted cheese plate

Grilled vegetables with grated Parmesan

Salad and Soup

Cream cheese bisque

Mixed baby greens with blue cheese crumbles

Main Course

Mixed cheese pie

Cheddar quiche

Dessert

Chocolate cheesecake

Mozzarella mousse

While I was finishing my meal, the door to the room crashed open, and a funny-looking sprite CARTWHEELED in. He was round and **potbellied** and had an intricate design of a clock face sewn onto his vest. He was wearing a pair of puffy pants with white-and-red stripes, and his skinny legs were covered by *green* tights.

On his head he wore a *green* jester's hat with three points that held three **jingling** golden bells. On his feet he wore flouncy gold slippers with bells that jingled as he walked. **"TA-DA!"** he sang in a squeaky voice as he cartwheeled up to me.

Ta-da!

THE EYES OF THE DRAGON OF TIME

"I am the **court jester**," the strange round sprite announced. "I will be your entertainment for the night! Thank you! Thank you very much!"

Then he pointed at me, laughing, "Hey, there's a **MOUSE** in the house! Thank you! Thank you very much!"

He ran toward me, **pirouetting** and shrieking, "Hey, Mousey, what's squeaking?!" When I tried to run off, he yanked me by the tail. "Come back! I'm just getting warmed up!"

Come back!

Eek! Let go!

I turned to Prince Lucky. "Who is this sprite?" I asked.

"His name is **Hee Haw**. His job is to make everyone laugh," he explained.

Hee Haw whirled around, making hilarious jumps. I had to admit — he was funny to watch.

But just then Hee Haw declared, "I need a volunteer!"

Before I could squeak, "Not me!" he ran toward me shrieking, "Think fast!" Then he tossed a cream pie in my face!

Oh, how that Hee Haw got on my nerves!

Hee, hee, hee!

Splat!

Everyone laughed. I didn't want to be a **BAD SPORT**, so I mumbled, "Heh, heh, good one."

"How about this one?" he 𝔰𝔫𝔦𝔠𝔨𝔢𝔯𝔢𝔡.

Then he tripped me. I fell flat on my face!

Oh, how that Hee Haw got on my nerves!

Next he pointed to the ground. I looked down. When I looked up, he poked me in the snout!

Oh, how that Hee Haw got on my nerves!

While everyone was laughing, Hee Haw spun around the room *faster* and *faster*. In fact, he was **spinning** so fast, just watching him

made me dizzy. I decided I needed a little fresh air, so I **tiptoed** over to the window and stared out. I saw blue sky, **puffy** clouds, a full moon, and . . . two enormouse *green* eyes!

"Help! There is a **MONSTER** at the window! Somebody do something!" I squeaked.

Everyone looked at me, astonished.

The sprites whispered, "Why is the knight so terrified?"

The gnomes whispered, "I thought he was brave."

The fairies whispered, "I thought he was **courageous**."

Peaclock flew over to the window and announced, "Those are the eyes of the DRAGON OF TIME, Knight."

Outside the castle window, suspended in midair, was an enormouse **DRAGON**. He had a clock hanging on a chain with 365 rings around his neck. His scales were **emerald green**, and there were twenty-four gems along his back to symbolize the hours of the day.

On his head he wore a crown that was covered with precious stones.

By now everyone, including the **DRAGON**, was staring at me. Of course they were wondering why a knight would make such a **FUSS** over a dragon. How embarrassing!

I didn't want to look like a fool, so I mumbled, "Well, of course, I knew those **EYES** belonged to a dragon. Knights and dragons go together like **mice** and **cheese**. I was just, um, making a joke."

The crowd continued to **stare** at me. Luckily, the prince came to my rescue. "Very funny, Knight. The Dragon of Time will be your guide to the Kingdom of the Witches! In this **CHEST** you will find directions to the Tower

of Fear and everything that you will need for the trip."

I climbed onto the saddle of the dragon, **grabbing** the reins with two paws. Even though I was scared out of my fur, I forced myself to sit up straight and yelled, "Ahem, I am off to save the Kingdom of Fan —"

But before I could finish the word *fantasy*, the Dragon of Time leaped into space. "*Heeeeeeelp!*" I squeaked.

And so I flew away from the Land of Time, leaving behind me a crowd full of doubts about why I was so *famouse* . . .

While the Dragon of Time flew between the stars, I promised myself that from that moment on, I would do my best to be brave.

After all, was I or was I not *Sir Geronimo of Stilton*, the fearless knight?

The only positive side to my leaving was that

I wouldn't have to deal with that annoying court jester.

Oh, how that Hee Haw got on my nerves!

As we soared **HIGHER** and **HIGHER** into the night sky, I tried to calm my jittery nerves by using some tips I had learned in a positive-thinking class. *Relax*, I told myself. *Take some nice deep breaths. So you are flying toward the Kingdom of the Witches. So it is a* **terrifying** *and highly* **DANGEROUS** *place from which few return. So the witches might tear out all your fur and leave you squeakless. So you may never see your family and friends again. That's no reason to worry . . .*

After three days and three nights of flying, I had talked myself into a complete and total panic attack! At last, on the fourth day, with the heat of the sun BURNING my fur (I knew I should have put on more sunscreen!), we reached the Kingdom of the Witches.

The Kingdom of the Witches

The Kingdom of the Witches

1. Petrified Peak
2. Wicked Witch Woods
3. Pale Ghost Peak
4. Lake of Tears
5. Greenhouse of Carnivorous Plants
6. River of Regret
7. Black Swamp
8. Restless Ghost Cemetery
9. Fanged Fish Farm
10. Moldy Mountain
11. Silent Sphinx Desert
12. Nightmare Forest
13. Fortress of Fear
14. Tower of Bones
15. Doom Door

ROTTED TEETH AND A FAKE NOSE!

We circled over the Kingdom of the Witches, passing through waves of dense fog. Below us, gnarled trees and thorny brambles blanketed the ground. Near the center of the kingdom stood the **TOWER OF BONES**, constructed by Eclipse. It was made of many, many bones and skulls. It had thirteen floors and POINTY windows that shone like unsettled eyes. On the top of the tower, there was a large burning fire. **SQUEAK!**

The dragon landed behind a thicket of brambles.

Lucky had told me that I would find everything necessary for the mission in the chest, so I got off the dragon and flipped it open. To my shock, out jumped **Hee Haw**, the pesky court jester!

"**Surprise!**" he shouted. "Happy to see me, Knight? I'm here to help!"

Needless to say, I was not happy at all. "I don't need your help. I'm on a very important mission here. I don't have time for your *silly* jokes," I argued.

But Hee Haw just pulled my whiskers and grinned. "Oh, come on, Knight. I know you're just a big old scaredy-mouse!" he insisted.

Then he pulled a scroll out of the chest. It had a note from Lucky on it.

Hee Haw read the letter, then said in a singsong

Dear Knight,

As soon as you see the Tower of Bones (I am sure that you will recognize it immediately), hide the dragon behind the Burning Thicket. (Be careful of the thorns. If they prick you . . . oh, how you'll burn!) Then disguise yourself as a witch to get inside unnoticed. In the chest, you will find everything you need. Good luck!

HERE ARE INSTRUCTIONS TO SEEM LIKE A REAL WITCH:

1. EAT WITH YOUR MOUTH OPEN. (Ew!)

2. PICK YOUR NOSE WITH YOUR FINGER. (Ew, ew!)

3. BURP A LOT. (Ew, ew, ew!)

4. TELL LIES. (The bigger they are the better!)

5. DANCE WITH THE OTHER WITCHES. (Even if you don't have a sense of rhythm!)

6. CAST SPELLS. (Or at least pretend!)

7. ABOVE ALL, BE UNKIND, VILLAINOUS, AND RUDE. (This is the most important thing!)

voice, "If you don't want to end up stuck in a ditch, just pretend that you're a mean old nasty WITCH!"

I was not too happy about having to dress up like a gross witch, but what could I do? I wanted to make it out of the kingdom *alive*!

With a deep sigh, I started getting dressed. First, I put on a worn black **dress** that went down to my feet. It was so dirty! Then, I put on black slippers that curled at the toes. I rubbed soot on my fur and put on a fake nose and bushy eyebrows. Then, I put a black wig on my head and added some fleas (yes, real ones!) that I found in a cage.

Finally, I put in fake yellow dentures with rotted teeth and chewed some garlic to make my breath stink. I plunked a black witch hat on my head and pinned a moon brooch to my dress. And last but not least, I grabbed a book of spells and a broom from the bottom of the chest.

Hee Haw snickered at my transformation. Then he poured a small vial of clear liquid over my head. Blech! Now I really stunk! I picked up the vial and read the label: **Witch Wonderful, For That Everyday Stink!** I was immediately encircled by a cloud of **flies**!

The court jester looked at me and announced, "Wow, we did it without a hitch! You are the **ugliest** scary old witch!"

I sighed. Oh yes, I looked disgusting . . .

But I was worried about one thing.

Would I be able to be **RUDE**? For me, that would be the most difficult part. After all, I am a gentlemouse!

From a fearless knight . . .

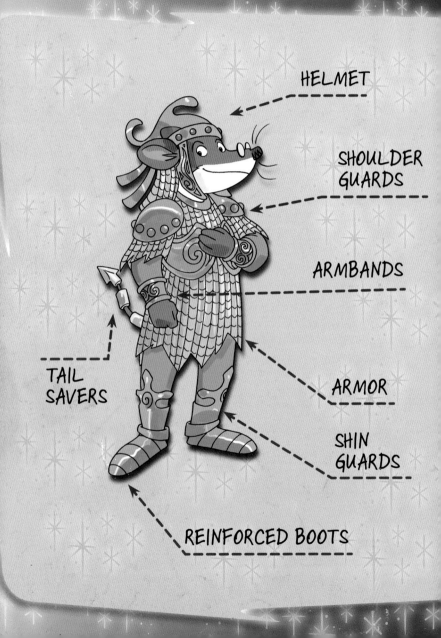

HELMET

SHOULDER GUARDS

ARMBANDS

ARMOR

SHIN GUARDS

TAIL SAVERS

REINFORCED BOOTS

... to a dirty, stinky witch!

FLEAS

BUSHY EYEBROWS

HAT

BROOM

WIG

GARLIC BREATH

WITCH DENTURES

FAKE NOSE

MAGIC BROOCH

BOOK OF MAGIC SPELLS

DIRTY BLACK DRESS

SLIPPERS

OH NO, I WON'T GO!

By the time I finished disguising myself, night had already fallen in that sad and **GLOOMY** place. Suddenly, I heard CACKLING laughs. I peeked out from behind the bramble bush and saw a long line of sneering witches carrying chopped wood. They were headed for the tower.

Besides the cackling, the witches **belched** and farted into the night. Their disgusting sounds

We'll cut down the trees!

We'll cut the trunks!

were amplified by the fierce **WIND OF THE WEST**. Witches these days! Hadn't they ever heard of a little thing called manners?

Unfortunately, the only way to enter the tower was to join the PROCESSION of witches. I thought Hee Haw would be coming with me, but he said, "Oh no, I won't go!"

Then he added, "Oh, and by the way, try to make it out alive! Otherwise, I'll have to go back alone!"

We have no regrets!   Let's cut it all down!

The **DRAGON OF TIME**, who was resting after the long and difficult flight, opened one eye. "Some kind of help you are. Shame on you for not supporting the knight!" he scolded.

Then he **turned** to me. "Sorry I cannot accompany you, Knight, but everyone would notice me with these **GREEN** scales and **long** tail and **GIANT** wings and

DRAGON head and . . . in other words, I'd stick out. Just know that I **believe** in you and I will be here for you — if you make it out! — and ready to fly away."

Then the dragon wrapped me in a **bone-crushing** hug with his humongous wing. "I know that you will make us proud! Good luck!" he said.

I believe in you!

I tried to squeak my thanks, but I was too busy gasping for air. I STUMBLED off into the night with my heart HAMMERING under my fur.

Not long after, I found myself on the path that led to the **TOWER OF FEAR**. With each pawstep, I heard a loud **crunch! Crunch! Crunch!** That's when

I realized the path I was headed down was not made of pebbles . . . it was made of **BONES**! Yikes!

And what a stink there was in the air! Of course, ahem, I didn't smell so great myself!

Inside, I was shaking like a leaf, but on the outside, I tried to look calm.

Soon I was surrounded by **WITCHES** of all types.

They greeted me cordially. "Hey you, old slipper,

what's your name? We haven't seen you around here!"

I responded with the first name that came to mind, "Ahem, my name is **GERONIMOSA WITCHYSNOUT**, but you can call me, um, Germy."

One of them patted me on the back. "I like your hat, Germy!"

Another sniffed me delightedly. "Wow, you reek, Germy! It smells like trash gone rancid! And look how many flies are flying around you!"

Another pulled a lock of my HAIR. "So greasy! I bet that you never wash it! Am I right, Germy? Am I right?"

Then they all began to sing and dance, and I was forced to imitate them . . .

QUEEN OF GLOOM AND DOOM

Under the full moon, the witches sang:

"Chop, chop the trees and plants!
We need wood for the fire!
The fire heats a boiling pot
filled with evil desire!
No, it's not a rotten soup;
it's evil wind we're making!
The wind grows stronger every day
and leaves the tower shaking!
Then one day soon we'll celebrate
with a stinky, slimy stew
because we will eliminate
revolting you-know-who!"

I turned to the witch next to me and asked, "Um, if you don't mind my asking, who is **you-know-who**?"

The witch, whose name was Mudsplatters, sneered. "Seriously, Germy? Did you just crawl out from under a cauldron? You-know-who is, of course, you know who, that foolish *Blossom of the Flowers*. Ugh! Just thinking about

her *sweet* flowery scent makes me want to puke!"

All the witches echoed, "It makes me want to puke!"

Another witch, **UGLYMUG**, pulled me aside and explained **ECLIPSE'S** evil plan. "You see this very tall tower? Up there, with a magic trap, Eclipse seizes the winds of the *Kingdom of Fantasy* and mixes them in a large pot put over a gigantic fire. In the pot, a very evil Wind of the West is created, then with her magic wand, she launches it at the Tick Tock Timepiece, making the hands turn more quickly."

Spiderleg, a witch who held a tarantula on a leash, cackled. "That's how we'll 'eliminate revolting you-know-who'!"

Thinking about Blossom made me want to **BURST** into tears, but I couldn't give away my cover. Luckily, none of the witches seemed to

notice my distress. I grabbed a load of wood and trudged along with the witches until we reached the **TOWER OF BONES**.

The procession of witches went down a corridor as dark as the belly of a hungry **CAT** and ended in a round room at the base of the tower. In the center, sitting on a throne of **sterling silver**, was a young witch with **disturbing** beauty. I say **disturbing** because she wasn't just beautiful — she was absolutely perfect. In fact, she was so perfect, she looked like a mannequin!

There wasn't one **wrinkle** or crease on her face. Her eyes were magnetic, like those of a cat, and her mouth looked like it had been painted by an artist. Her hair was purple and **shiny** with thick wavy curls that reached the floor.

On her head was a silver crown adorned with a giant white **pearl** in the shape of a skull.

She wore a black velvet dress, and around her

ECLIPSE THE WITCH

NAME: Eclipse, the Witch of Darkness; also called Queen of Gloom and Doom; Ruler of Bad Choices, Evil Things, and All-Around Badness

RESIDENCE: Lives in the Tower of Bones, an evil building made of many skulls and bones. It has thirteen floors and pointy windows.

SPECIAL ACCESSORY: She always wears a large, shiny pendant in the shape of a full moon and a silver crown adorned with an enormous pearl in the shape of a skull.

SECRET DREAM: She would like to steal the beauty of Blossom, the Queen of the Fairies, and rule the Kingdom of Fantasy in her own terrifying way!

FAVORITE MOTTO: "Don't worry, be gloomy!"

neck hung a silver **MEDALLION** in the shape of a full moon.

In her right hand, she gripped a silver magic wand that was connected to her wrist with a silver chain. Even her shoes seemed to be made of **sterling silver**. How strange. Who could walk in metal shoes?

While the witches danced and sang around her, her face remained expressionless. Then, suddenly, she raised an arm and shrieked, "**Sileeence!** I, Eclipse, the Witch of Darkness; Queen of Gloom and Doom; Ruler of Bad Choices, Evil Things, and All-Around Badness, have something to say!"

My eyes bulged in surprise — while Eclipse looked young, her voice was **raspy** and deep, like that of someone much older!

TWO OF THE WITCHES ARE TWINS. CAN YOU SPOT THEM?

Hee, hee, hee!

SOLUTION: The twin witches are both near the bottom of the picture, one on the left and one near the center. They are each wearing purple hats, purple jackets, green belts, and green skirts.

NOT ME!

Eclipse leaned forward in her chair and demanded, "Whoever knows how to READ and **WRITE**, step forward immediately!"

All the witches looked at one another, puzzled. One by one they shrugged and said, *"not me!"*

One witch named Ditzy spoke up. "Your Evilness, why would we want to read and write? How boring."

Eclipse threw one of her **sterling silver** slippers at Ditzy and yelled, "Quiet, you! Did I ask for your opinion?"

Just then a short, chubby witch named Greenmuck (who smelled like swamp mud and had a dress made of braided algae) pushed me from behind.

"Hey, how about the new witch, Germy?! She

must know how to read — she's got a *book* under her arm!"

I **STUMBLED** in my curly slippers as she pushed me and landed right on my snout on the black marble floor!

SMACK!

All the witches began **rolling** on the floor with laughter. "Ha, ha, ha! Germy can read, and

How about the new witch?

Oof!

she's a clown! Ha, ha, ha! What a strange witch!"

The only one who didn't laugh was Eclipse. She walked toward me, **STARING** at me intensely. "You! Do you really know how to read and write? Come forward, and don't waste my time!" she instructed.

I hurried to curtsy, answering in a high-pitched voice, "Yes, **Your Wickedness**, I am at your service!"

She passed me a scroll and ordered, "If you can read, then tell me what is written here."

I polished my glasses, cleared my throat, and read aloud:

"Spell Number Thirteen:
How to become young and beautiful again.
If an old and ugly witch wants —"

But before I could continue, she **SWIPED** the scroll from my paws, shouting, "Enough! What's wrong with you — reading my private

documents in front of everyone?"

I wanted to point out that she was the one who had asked me to read **ALOUD** in the first place, but that didn't seem like a good idea, so I kept silent.

At that moment, she grabbed me by the neck and declared, "You will become the new *librarian* of the Tower of Bones! You will put all the books in the witch library in **ALPHABETICAL ORDER**, which should take a century at least. The rest of you, get back to work. I need more wood for the fire!"

All the witches poured back outside, singing:

"Chop, chop, chop the wood.

Spreading evil is all good!

There is still much work to do

to steal the life from you-know-who!"

Puff . . . pant . . . wait for me . . .

The witch library was at the very **top** of the tower. By the time I had followed Eclipse up the 313 steps that led there, I was **huffing** and PUFFING like the Rodent's Express Train!

POT OF THE WICKED WINDS

After I stopped **panting**, I looked around. I expected to see a stuffy old witch library, but what I saw made . . .

my whiskers tremble with fear!
my paws shake!
MY FUR STAND ON END!

In addition to the library, the top floor of the tower was also Eclipse's laboratory! And I thought just seeing all those **SPOOKY** witch books would make my heart hammer!

The room was enormouse and circular. The floor was made of gray **stone** slabs inlaid with silver stars. The ceiling was made completely out of crystal, and you could see the dark, *eerie* sky above.

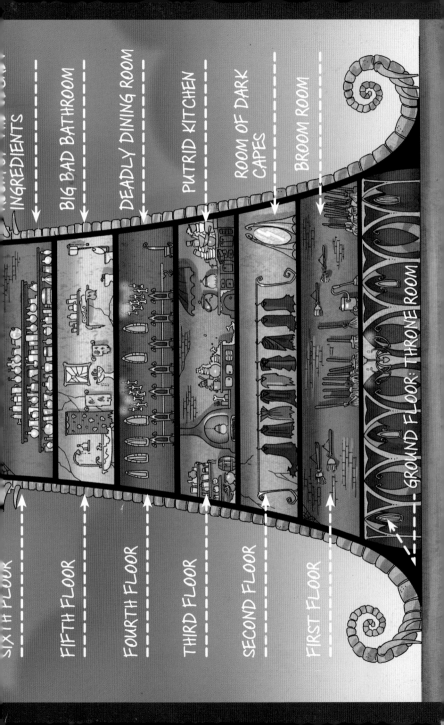

In the center of the room, there was a crackling fire. On the fire sat an enormouse silver pot that was as large as the heated SWIMMING pool in my uncle Richrat's backyard. There was writing engraved on the pot. It said: *Pot of the Wicked Winds*. The pot was so tall that whoever was stirring it would have to climb up the silver staircase perched next to it!

From the pot came a strong *swirling wind* that made my whiskers whirl. It was the terrible Wind of the West! Next to the pot rested a long copper spoon with a SUN on its handle and a large fork with a **moon** on its handle.

I guess Eclipse must have had a

thing for stargazing, because a super-size **telescope** pointed up at the ominous sky.

Only then did I notice all the **astronomy** books.

That witch had an incredible library!

Eclipse went to a window, leaned out, and pulled up a net made of **sparkling** silver thread. She emptied the net into the pot, and a mass of mixed winds came out. Then she blew on the pot with her stinky breath. **Pee-yew**!

As the witch stirred, she muttered to herself, "Boiled bugs breath! If I stop stirring for one minute, these winds get all **crusted** and tangled!"

Then she called to me. "You, Germy, come here and **stir**! And be careful not to let clumps of

wind form on the bottom, understand? Or I will transform you into a **tadpole**! I just decided that in addition to working as a librarian, you will also be my **wind mixer**."

I swallowed hard and hurried to obey. "I will stir with all my strength, Your Evilness!"

I climbed up and looked into the pot. All the winds mixed together, forming a violent and **smelly** current of air.

The witch, meanwhile, kicked off her silver shoes, sending them **clattering** to the floor.

Then she snorted. "Ugh, those metal shoes are killing me! They're worse than my four-inch **PLATFORM** batwing boots!"

Eclipse went over to the **DARKEST** corner of the laboratory and collapsed on a chair that looked like a throne. She lit a candelabra, opened a golden chest locked with a key, and began to study a series of **scrolls**. "Hmm . . . spy mirror . . . hmm . . . magic sauté . . ." she mumbled.

Perched on her left shoulder was an owl with yellow eyes named **BLiNKERS**, and above her head, suspended from the chair, was a purple bat named **SCREECH**. On the arm of the chair stood a **BLUE** spider.

How strange! I had never seen a blue spider before. Even **stranger**, this spider wore a little **crown** on his head and a little chain attached to one of his legs.

But I had no time to think about that spider. I had work to do in the library. The place was a colossal

Hmm . . .

mess! I began to put all the books in **alphabetical** order.

There were thousands of books! Eclipse wasn't kidding — this job would take me **centuries** to complete!

While I was shelving the books, I kept thinking about Blossom. I had to figure out a way to **COUNTERACT** Eclipse's spell that was producing the *Wind of the West*.

How did she even capture the **wicked winds** in the large pot? Maybe the answer was in the scrolls she was studying . . .

Quiet as a mouse, I approached the scrolls to take a little peek.

But **ECLIPSE** saw me and swiped at me with her broom, shrieking, "Get lost, spy! If I catch you touching my secret scrolls again, I'll cut off your paw!"

The owl pecked me, hooting, "**Shove off, witch!**"

The bat flapped in my face, screeching, "Shoo, Stinky!"

Only the blue spider said nothing.

SPELL NUMBER 14

After a while, Eclipse dozed off on the chair and began to snore loudly. "Zzzz . . . zzzz . . . zzzz . . . zzzz!" What a racket!

A few minutes later, the blue spider crawled up to me and whispered in my ear, "You must be **CAREFUL**, witch! Do you know how many librarians Eclipse has already turned into tadpoles?"

He pointed to a fishbowl filled with **tadpoles** swimming around dejectedly. Cheese niblets!

Then the spider reassured me with a **kind** tone. "But don't

worry, I will help you. My name is Webster. I am the king of the Blue Spiders."

I shook his little foot and squeaked, "Pleased to meet you. My name is Stil — I mean, Geronimosa Witchysnout. But, please, call me Germy."

The spider smiled. He told me that Eclipse was the most evil of her seven sisters.

"She has sisters?" I asked.

Nice to meet you!

I am Webster, the king of the Blue Spiders!

Webster looked at me curiously. "How come you don't know this, Germy? Even the youngest witch knows about the sisters," he pointed out. "I mean, if you weren't hideously ugly and your breath wasn't disgustingly stinky and you weren't dressed in black with a pointy hat, I'd say you're not a witch!"

I hurried to respond. "Ahem, of course I am a REAL witch! I even have a broom."

The spider pointed at a frame on the wall with paintings of the seven witch sisters! Of the witches, I immediately recognized Cackle, whom I had already met on several previous trips to the Kingdom of Fantasy.

Cackle and ECLIPSE are sisters! Yikes!

I didn't want Webster to know, but those witches terrified me! "So, listen, what are all those moldy scrolls Eclipse is studying?" I asked the spider, trying to forget about Cackle.

CACKLE
the most ambitious

ECLIPSE
the smartest

FRIGID
the most coldhearted

VENDETTA
the most vindictive

STENCH
the stinkiest

EERIE
the darkest

SHADOW
the most mysterious

Webster sighed. "They are the **Bewitching Scrolls**. Don't ever touch them if you value your life and don't want to turn into a bag of bones, or a squashed lump with whiskers, or a sad starving skeleton in a witch dress, or . . ."

He was about to go on, but I held up my paw. "I get the idea," I whispered, horrified.

Webster showed me the SiLVeR CHAiN attached to his little leg. "See this?" he said. "Eclipse is keeping me hostage. She has enslaved the entire **BLue SPiDeR** population!"

I was shocked. "What does she make you do?"

The spider lowered his voice. "She makes us weave an invisible net, which she uses to snare all the wicked winds in the Kingdom of the Witches. She uses spell *Number Fourteen* from the **Bewitching Scrolls**!"

My eyes opened wide. Finally, the mystery was beginning to unravel. Eclipse used spell *Number 14* to create the wicked Wind of the West!

At last I knew what I had to do. I had to get my paws on those Bewitching Scrolls without being turned into a **bag of bones**!

SPYING MIRROR, TELL ME THE LATEST!

As I spent more time with the witches, I realized that there was only one moment of each day when Eclipse was **BUSY** and no one else would bother me in the laboratory. It was early in the morning. Eclipse would disappear behind a silver door labeled SECRET ROOM, locking it with a loud **CLICK**. Meanwhile, her owl was still out hunting prey, and the bat was still in a deep sleep, hanging on his **GOLDEN** perch.

That was when I could examine the **Bewitching Scrolls**!

So one morning I waited, pretending to put the witch's books in order.

As soon as she went into the SECRET ROOM, I put my eye up to the keyhole. What I

saw made my blood run cold!

The witch held a silver mirror decorated with precious **RUBIES**.

Blistering blue cheese! It was identical to the one that I had seen in Blossom's hands before I left! The witch ordered, "Spying Mirror, tell me the latest news!"

The mirror laughed, then began to speak. "Well, let's see . . . this morning Blossom got up at six, had a sip of dew for breakfast, washed her hair with a HONEYSUCKLE and rose petal rinse, then practiced some peaceful meditation . . ."

The witch interrupted, "You foolish piece of glass! Those details don't interest me — tell me if she has become **older** and uglier!"

The mirror hurried to show her an image of Blossom, even more wrinkled and tired.

The witch cackled, satisfied. "Excellent! My plan is working! The Wind of the West continues to

make the Timepiece's hands turn, and little M̲i̲s̲s̲
G̲o̲o̲d̲y̲ T̲w̲o̲-S̲h̲o̲e̲s̲ ages by the minute!"

Then Eclipse began to sing:

*"I want your youth.
I want your looks.
I'll get it all
with my spell books!
It's my turn now
to rule it all;
The kingdom is mine
after you fall!"*

Thinking of Blossom made me want to C̲R̲Y̲.
I had to save her!

1. I approached the scrolls . . .

2. Then I began to go through them, keeping an eye on the door . . .

3. But I was too nervous! How stressful!

Suddenly, the door to the SECRET ROOM burst open, and Eclipse ran out, heading for the stairs.

"I'm going to my room to rest. I don't want to be disturbed, understand?" she yelled before DISAPPEARING.

This was it! I ran to examine the **Bewitching Scrolls**.

Leafing through them, I grew more and more anxious. What if someone discovered me?! With one **EYE**, I tried to read, and with the other **EYE**, I tried to see if the witch was coming. With my left **ear**, I tried to listen for the owl, and with my right **ear**, I tried to hear if the bat had woken up . . .

It was so stressful! I couldn't handle the pressure!

YOU'RE A WITCH, NOT A FAIRY!

My whole body was *trembling*. *Get a grip, Stilton!* I told myself. *Think calm thoughts. Imagine you're in a peaceful place like a beautiful beach or a lush green forest. The beach is warm and sunny, and the forest doesn't have any unfriendly creatures like terrifying trolls or wicked witches or giant mouse-eating boa constrictors . . .* Okay, maybe thinking wasn't such a good idea.

Now, where was I? Oh yes, eventually I came upon a scroll labeled *Spell Number 13*. After I read it, I was **SCARED** out of my fur!

Spell numbers 14, 15, 16, 45, and 87 were no **Picnic**, either. Oh, what a nightmare!

How to Become Young and Beautiful

If an old and ugly witch wishes to become young and beautiful, there is only one solution: Steal youth and beauty from another creature, possibly a fairy!

Note: The most fascinating fairy is Blossom of the Flowers, but in her case, the only way to steal her gifts would be to accelerate the hands of the Tick Tock Timepiece, the clock that measures her life and that of all of the Kingdom of Fantasy. Every witch has always dreamed of doing it, but no one has ever succeeded.

P.S. If a witch ever succeeds, let us know so we can update the spells!

How to Create the Wind of the West

To generate this wind, which has the strength of a hurricane, one needs to make the Magic Sauté in a large pot (see ingredients in Spell Number 15). Then add all the winds that you can capture, one at a time. Capturing the wicked winds is difficult but not impossible (see explanation in Spell Number 16). After exactly thirteen hours of cooking, the magic mixture will produce the Wind of the West.

Pot of the Wicked Winds

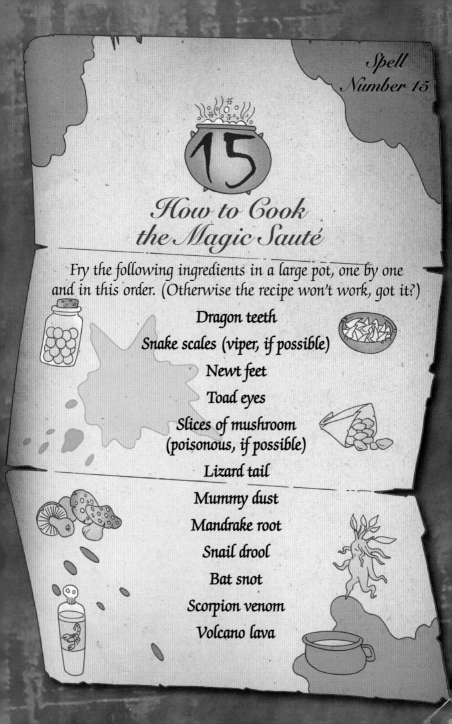

How to Cook
the Magic Sauté

Fry the following ingredients in a large pot, one by one and in this order. (Otherwise the recipe won't work, got it?)

Dragon teeth

Snake scales (viper, if possible)

Newt feet

Toad eyes

Slices of mushroom
(poisonous, if possible)

Lizard tail

Mummy dust

Mandrake root

Snail drool

Bat snot

Scorpion venom

Volcano lava

16

How to Capture the Wicked Winds of the Kingdom of the Witches

The first thing you must do is persuade the population of Blue Spiders to weave a spiderweb with spider tears, well soaked with their pain and sadness. This spiderweb is the only one that can trap the wind! In order for this spell to work, the web must be full of excruciating pain. While the spiders weave, they must cry — the sadder they are, the better it is! One way to obtain this result would be to kidnap their king and keep him hostage.

How to Spy on Your Nemesis without Her Realizing It

Simple: You need two Spying Mirrors made of sterling silver and decorated with very precious rubies.

Send one of the Spying Mirrors to your nemesis and keep the other. Yours will reflect everything that happens to your nemesis. (If she gets a zit on her nose, you will be the first to know it!) In fact, the mirror has the capacity to see and listen, telling you everything, even if at a great distance!

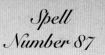

How to Transform the Librarian into a Tadpole
(If She Doesn't Work Hard Enough!)

This is very simple. Hit her on the head with your magic wand and say, "Ugly Witch, you're way too slow, into the goldfish bowl you go!" Suddenly, she will transform into a tadpole, and you can plop her into a bowl of stinky water.

Now I was **HORRIFIED**. This evil magic practically made this witch invincible! There was only one way to fight her. I had to find an even **MORE POWERFUL** spell!

But that seemed so impossible, I began to sob.

Without thinking, I wailed, "Now I'll never be able to save Queen Blossom!"

Right then Webster appeared by my side, dragging his CHAIN. Oops! I had forgotten about the spider. "Blossom?" he said. "How do you know her, Germy? You're a witch, not a **fairy**!"

Then he stared at me and **murmured**, "Hey, wait a second, I never noticed you had whiskers just like a **MOUSE**. And a nose just like a **MOUSE**. And aren't those the ears of a **MOUSE**?"

Ah, well. I guess my witch disguise wasn't foolproof. Webster grinned now that he knew my true identity. "I knew you were too **nice** to be a wicked witch!" he exclaimed.

"You're too kind," I said, **BLUSHING** modestly. What can I say? Even when I'm dressed up as a witch, I can't help behaving like a *gentlemouse*!

"I will tell you a **secret**," Webster said, handing me a scroll. "This is the most powerful spell of the Bewitching Scrolls: Number One Thousand. With this spell, you can cancel all the other spells executed by Eclipse!"

Quickly, I read *Spell Number 1,000*.

Finally, I had found a way to **SAVE** Blossom!

Thanks, Webster!

Here is the most powerful spell!

1,000

How to Cancel Spells

Close your eyes, plug your nose with
your right hand, pull your left ear with
your left hand, stick out your tongue,
and say out loud:

"Witches with wands, warlocks
with bats,

poisonous spiders, rabid black cats!

Cancel the spells that are
already done;

Terminate all spells, every
last one!"

POISONOUS SPIDERS, RABID BLACK CATS

I raced over to the *Pot of the Wicked Winds*. There was no time to lose! I climbed up the silver stairs and stared into the pot.

Inside, the stinky mixture was bubbling and **boiling** as it blended together to form the evil *Wind of the West*.

Holding on to my pointy hat so I didn't get blown away, I closed my **EYES** (or did I need to keep them open?), then I plugged my nose with the right paw (or was it supposed to be the left?). I pulled my left ear (or was it the right?), I **STUCK** out my tongue, and said aloud the magic words:

"Witches with wands, warlocks with bats . . ."

Witches with wands . . .

Pot of the
Wicked
Winds

SECRET
ROOM

And then I stopped. Rats! I forgot how the spell went!

I ran back and reopened the chest, but the wind **LIFTED** **Yaaawn!** the scrolls into the air. I tried to

Hoot!

catch them, but right then Blinkers the owl began to **BEAT** on the window for someone to let him in, and Screech the bat *yawned*, slowly waking up!

I also heard the footsteps of Eclipse click-clack on the stairs as she approached!

"Hurry," Webster urged. *"Or everything will be lost!"*

I tried again, filled with panic.

"Um, cats and poisonous wands,

bats and rabid spells . . ."

I heard the witch behind me yell **furiously**, "Who dared to touch my Bewitching Scrolls?"

At this point I wanted to jump into the boiling pot and call it a day, but I couldn't do that to Blossom. I had to keep trying. So I did. And this time I got the words right!

"Witches with wands, warlocks with bats, poisonous spiders, rabid black cats! Cancel the spells that are already done; Terminate all spells, every last one!"

Just like that, the Wind of the West lost **Power** and vanished.

I had completed my mission!

But before I could celebrate, I heard an **icy** voice behind me . . .

Full of **terror**, I turned and saw that a few inches from my snout was the wrinkle-free face of Eclipse.

She stared at me with her **icy** eyes that showed no emotion and hissed, "Well, well, well, who do we have here? So you aren't an ugly **witch**; you're an ugly **MOUSE** spy . . ."

She raised her silver wand high, threatening me. "You were able to **STOP** the Wind of the West, but I will get revenge. Now you will feel my power. Whatever you have heard about me, I am much, much **WORSE**!"

She came closer and **HISSED**, "Maybe I will transform you into a warty toad! Or I will lock you in a dark prison for a thousand millennia! Or I will throw you into the *Pot of the Wicked Winds*! Tell me your name, so I can have it carved on your **HEADSTONE**, if I even decide to give you a headstone . . ."

But as Eclipse continued to shriek I realized something strange was happening. Wrinkles were sprouting up all over her face. Her nose **shriveled**, and her chin sagged. Her hair went from shiny purple to *frizzy* white, and her back became stooped.

OOPS. I FORGOT . . .

"It worked! Spell Number One Thousand canceled all the spells done before! And Eclipse is returning to her cranky, **OLD** witchy self! Well, she was always cranky, but now she's wrinkling back up like a prune," Webster yelled happily.

I was so excited! If Eclipse was getting **older**, that meant Blossom was getting younger!

Yes, everything was working exactly how I had hoped! But a minute later, disaster struck. The **MARBLE** floor began to creak, the walls began to shift, and the whole Tower of Bones began to crumble!

"Oops," Webster **MUMBLED**. "I forgot to mention . . . the Tower of Bones was also constructed with a **SPELL**."

Now, that was a piece of **information** that would

have come in handy! I groaned. Still, I didn't want to make Webster feel bad, so I grabbed him, put him in my pocket, and started running.

As I raced down the stairs, I counted the floors . . .

Ahhhhh!

Run, run!

"Thirteenth floor, TWELFTH floor, ELEVENTH floor, tenth floor, ninth floor . . ."

But just as we passed the eighth floor, I found myself in front of a giant gaping hole in the stairs. If I tried to take one more pawstep, I was a goner, just like the crumbling Tower of Bones!

Oh, what to do, what to do, what to doooo?!

I was hoping some brilliant idea would come to me, but nothing did. So I stuck my head out the window and squeaked,

"Heeeeeeeeeeeeeeeelp!"

It was right then that I saw the most incredible sight I could imagine . . .

The DRAGON OF TIME was hurtling through the sky, heading straight for me!

The dragon wagged his tail to let me know that he had seen me. But who was in the saddle, holding the reins?

It was Hee Haw!

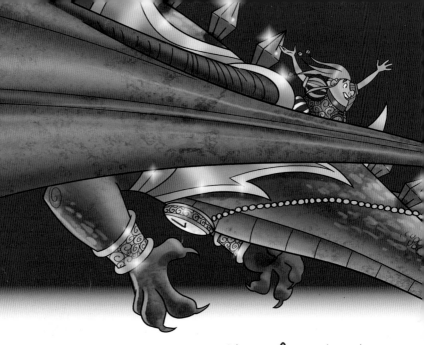

He yelled triumphantly, "Never fear, Hee Haw is here!"

The dragon accelerated and was soon right in front of me.

Hee Haw reached for me with his hand, and I took it, just as the **TOWER OF BONES** fell to the ground, raising a cloud of dust. I sank onto the dragon right behind Hee Haw.

"Congratulations, Knight! You have succeeded in completing your mission!" the dragon cheered.

I felt like I was on TOP of the world! (Well, technically I was on top of the dragon!) It felt so good to have saved Blossom! I thanked Hee Haw for his help. Who would have thought that pesky court jester would play a part in **saving** my life! "Don't thank me, Knight! I knew we'd be tight!" he snickered, **bopping** me on the nose. Ah, well, some things never change.

Webster was celebrating in my pocket, too . . . But then I spotted Eclipse on her **BROOMSTICK**. What did she want?

NOT SO FAST, MOUSEY!

The witch hung in the air with her broom vibrating. She held up one **gnarled** hand and cackled, "Not so fast, Mousey! I'm not done with you yet!"

The bat yelled, "Yeah, you don't have all the **facts**!"

And the owl added, "That's right. There's more to the **story**!"

Uh-oh. What was the witch up to now?

The Dragon of Time echoed my fears. "The witch must be planning some other way to **rule** the kingdom."

Hee Haw shook his head and sighed, **bonking** me in the eye with the jingling bell on his hat. "I was just glad, but now I'm sad!" he complained.

The witch shrieked, "You haven't won, because . . .

**EVEN THOUGH YOU STOPPED
THE WIND OF THE WEST . . .**

AND CRUSHED THE TOWER OF BONES . . .

**YOU CAN'T DESTROY THE LAYER OF
DARKNESS, BECAUSE THAT IS NOT THE WORK
OF A MAGIC SPELL. IT IS THE WORK OF
THE BLUE SPIDERS! HA, HA, HAAA!"**

Ha, ha, ha!

Ha, ha, ha!

Ha, ha, ha!

I didn't know what Eclipse was talking about, but before I could ask, she started flying away. "Get ready, Mouse!" she yelled over her shoulder. "In **three** days, there will be an ECLIPSE of the moon. That is when you lose it all!"

The witch aimed her broom directly toward the ground. Then she pointed her magic wand at a white stone in the shape of a skull.

"Doom Door, open up . . . or else!"

The white stone slowly rose, revealing a **DARK** tunnel. Eclipse flew right into the

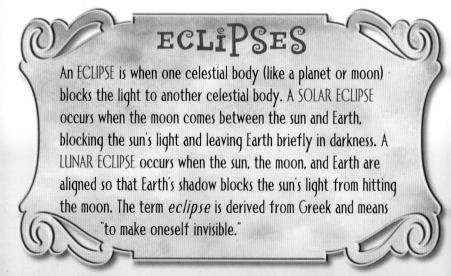

ECLIPSES

An ECLIPSE is when one celestial body (like a planet or moon) blocks the light to another celestial body. A SOLAR ECLIPSE occurs when the moon comes between the sun and Earth, blocking the sun's light and leaving Earth briefly in darkness. A LUNAR ECLIPSE occurs when the sun, the moon, and Earth are aligned so that Earth's shadow blocks the sun's light from hitting the moon. The term *eclipse* is derived from Greek and means "to make oneself invisible."

tunnel and disappeared!

Questions swirled around in my brain like clothes *tumbling* in a dryer. "What just happened?" I squeaked, terrified. "Where did the witch go? Why did she say I would lose it all? What is the **LAYER OF DARKNESS**? What will happen in three days? Why does the ECLIPSE of the moon matter?"

I was so filled with questions, I felt like I was about to explode.

Webster explained that the witch's Doom Door led to her underground crypt. "That's where Eclipse has imprisoned all the other BLue SpiDeRS! After they made the invisible net, she's now forcing them to weave the **LAYER OF DARKNESS**. It can darken the sky of the Kingdom of Fantasy forever. She's planning on using it in three days, when there will be a lunar eclipse."

THE LONG-LEGGED HISTORY OF THE BLUE SPIDERS

Once upon a time, the Blue Spiders lived peacefully in an immense underground lair in the Valley of the Long Legs. There they lived happily, weaving their beautiful webs.

Then, one terrible day, the evil witch Eclipse invaded the valley and kidnapped their king, Websteronius B. Weaver, also known as Webster. So the Blue Spiders were imprisoned in a cave, where they became the slaves of Eclipse!

Using Spell Number 16 from the Bewitching Scrolls, Eclipse forced them to weave a gigantic invisible net. The net was woven with the tears of the spiders, soaked with their sadness. The witch used the net to capture the Wind of the West, made up of all the winds in the Kingdom of the Witches. Now the Blue Spiders are being forced to weave another net called the Layer of Darkness. With this net, the witch plans to darken the sun forever and rule the Kingdom of Fantasy.

Webster waved one long leg in the air (or was it his hand? It's hard to tell with a spider). "We must **STOP** the witch and save my subjects!" he declared. "But first let me tell you about the history of the BLUE SPIDERS . . ."

Listening to Webster's story about the imprisoned spiders made me feel sad and **MAD** and SCARED all at the same time. I was sad because I felt bad for the spiders, of course. Who would want to live underground, WEAVING your little legs off day in and day out? I felt mad because I could just picture that nasty selfish witch ordering the poor Blue Spiders around. And I felt scared because I knew the only way to help the spiders would be to **confront** the witch! Did I mention I'm a bit of a scaredy-mouse? I'm deathly afraid of witches, dark places, scorpions, and SLEEPING BAGS. I once got my tail fur stuck in my sleeping bag zipper! Ouch!

But that's another **story** . . .

Anyway, we all agreed that we had to act **QUICKLY** to stop the witch from executing her evil plan.

"We need some sort of **SPECIAL** weapon," Webster suggested. "Something tough enough to cut through the Layer of Darkness. But I have no idea what. The fabric is super-resistant."

The **DRAGON OF TIME** spoke up. "I know of an object that could cut through the **LAYER OF DARKNESS**. But it will be incredibly difficult to get."

"We have to try," I said. "It's our only hope!"

Hee Haw nodded in agreement, bonking me again with his **jingling** bells. **BONK!** Oh, why couldn't he switch to a nice **soft** knit cap instead? Maybe he could ask Blossom for one for his birthday . . .

The Dragon of Time interrupted my thoughts.

"In the *Kingdom of Fantasy*, there is something called the Crystal Sword. It is an enchanted sword with legendary powers. The blade is polished with stardust, sharpened with moonstones, and washed with fairy tears."

"Where do we find it?" I asked.

The dragon sighed. "That's the problem. The sword belongs to KING AZUL, who lives in SAPPHIRE CITY. The sword could be

THE CRYSTAL SWORD

The Crystal Sword is an enchanted sword with legendary powers. Its blade, sharpened with moonstones and shined with stardust, gets its power from fairy tears. It can cut through any material: superhard, supersoft, or even super-sticky!

dangerous if it falls into the wrong hands, so the king keeps it guarded in a remote place known as **SHRIEK PEAK.**"

"I know Azul — I met him on my sixth trip to the *Kingdom of Fantasy*!" I squeaked.

TELL ME SOMETHING
I DON'T KNOW

We traveled all day and night on the back of the Dragon of Time until we saw Shining Moon Mountain. We flew up Shriek Peak and finally arrived at SAPPHIRE CITY, the city in the clouds, right as the warm rays of the sun tinted the clouds gold. Here is where we would find AZUL, the Ancient One with Eyes of Sapphire.

The dragon landed outside the confines of the city and stayed there to wait for us. After I had put on my armor (what a relief it was to take off that stinky witch disguise!), Hee Haw, Webster, and I set out for the palace. There we met seven knights dressed in the seven colors of the RAINBOW.

"We are the *honorable guards* of Azul!

Please, follow us. Azul is waiting for you!" declared the knights.

That was odd. **HOW** did the king know we were coming?

As we walked through that *spectacular* city made of clouds, my paws sank into the soft ground. It was like walking on **marshmallows**! We passed lots of **fancy** houses, but eventually we stopped in front of a **simple** dwelling. This was Azul's house. The wise ruler knew that it's not the **size** of the house that counts — it's

Here we are in Sapphire City!

those inside that matter most!

Inside, Azul was sitting on a simple WOODEN chair. He wore a long white tunic, which, I must admit, reminded me of my aunt Sweetfur's bathRobe. His eyes were as blue as sapphires.

Even though I had met the king before, I still felt nervous. Azul was one impressive ruler! He was famouse in the Kingdom of Fantasy for his profound **wisdom**.

Azul, the Ancient One with Eyes of Sapphire

WHO HE IS: The ancient and wise leader of Sapphire City

RESIDENCE: Sapphire City, the city in the clouds. His house is the most modest in the whole city, and on his door these words are engraved: ALL ARE WELCOME HERE!

FAMILY: He is the father of Blue Rider, the knight who helped Geronimo in his sixth trip to the Kingdom of Fantasy.

SPECIAL ACCESSORY: A long, golden scepter with a large, sparkly sapphire at the top

FAVORITE MOTTO: Love conquers all!

I bowed before the king. "I'm not sure if you remember me. I am Stilton, er, *Geronimo*, um, a mouse — or, rather, a knight . . ." I mumbled.

Azul interrupted, saying kindly, "I know."

"Oh, well, I am here because . . ." I began again.

"I know," the king said once again.

I blinked, confused. Until I remembered then that Azul had the **magical** ability to read minds! He knew exactly what I was thinking! I **blushed**, wondering if he caught my thoughts about his outfit.

Azul addressed me warmly. "My dear Sir Geronimo of Stilton, how could I forget you?! You will always have a **home** here. Oh, and don't worry about it. I know my robe looks a little funny, but I must tell you, it is so **comfy**!"

By now I was as **RED** as a tomato. Oh, how embarrassing!

Azul continued, "Please, speak freely. I will listen."

So I said, "The witch **ECLIPSE** . . . but maybe you already know. She has the **LAYER OF DARKNESS** . . . but maybe you already know. We need to cut it before the ECLIPSE of the moon . . . but maybe you already know. And so

I will listen!

The witch . . . the Layer of Darkness . . .

we need the CRYSTAL SWORD . . . but maybe you already know."

Azul nodded **tranquilly** with his gaze fixed on mine. Then he closed his eyes, and for a minute I wondered if he had *dozed* off.

Finally, his eyes slowly opened, and he said, "In fact, I already knew." I wasn't surprised. "Now tell me something I don't know. Tell me the answer to the RIDDLE OF THE ENCHANTED POMEGRANATE, and the Crystal Sword is yours!"

Then he stood up and said, "*FOLLOW ME!*"

TEMPTING . . .
VERY TEMPTING . . .

We climbed aboard a CRYSTAL carriage, pulled by three *winged* unicorns.

The carriage flew up Shriek Peak, the tallest mountain in the Kingdom of Fantasy. *Don't look down!* I warned myself, **clinging** to the side of the carriage for dear life.

When we landed, Azul pointed at a RiDDLe engraved on a plaque of ice:

RIDDLE OF THE ENCHANTED POMEGRANATE

A special sword rests on this peak:
A blade with powers so unique.
But only one can claim its hold:
A fearless knight (or so it's told).
To find it, you must choose a path.
One, two, or three: You do the math.

Azul then pointed out **three** paths that branched in front of us and instructed me to choose one.

I looked at the three roads. They were very different.

At the start of the first road, there was a shiny gold sign. It read: *Road to Riches*. It was paved with golden coins, and I could see piles of precious, glittering gemstones along the path. If I walked down that road, I could pick up more money than the wealthiest mouse on Mouse Island. I could move out of my modest mouse hole and into a *mansion*! It was tempting . . . very tempting . . .

On the second road was a shiny silver sign that read: **Bragger's Boulevard**. It was paved with **mirrors**, and under every mirror was written a little saying like, "You are better than everyone!" and "The whole world is **jealous** of you!" and "You are perfect in every way!"

If I chose that road I would be the most **CONFIDENT** mouse on the block. It might be nice to think so highly of myself. It was tempting . . . very tempting . . . .

The sign above the third road was made out of old wood. It read: SiMPLe STReeT. There were no gold coins or shiny mirrors on this path. It was made of plain dirt and stones and had narrow unequal steps.

I stood silent, staring at the three paths.

Which one should I take?

I knew my decision could either lead me to the CRYSTAL SWORD or to disaster. Oh, why did these adventures always force me to make so many decisions? I had trouble even deciding between a cheese bagel and a cheese sandwich!

I turned to Azul, hoping he could guide me, but he refused to make eye contact. I had to make this decision on my own.

Once more I looked at the three roads. Then suddenly it **HIT** me. I was a simple mouse. I had to be true to myself and take the simplest path. So without any more hesitating I took off down SiMPLe STReet until I found myself in front of the most wonderful sight. A giant POMEGRANATE made entirely of precious stones! The skin was made of red rubies, the tree it grew on was made of diamonds, and the leaves were shiny **emeralds**.

Slowly, the enchanted pomegranate opened into four pieces. And, there, in the very center of the fruit sat the CRYSTAL SWORD!

I took a step forward and grabbed the sword.

I did it! I had chosen the right path!

No Messenger Service Required

At last, the Crystal Sword, otherwise known as the *Sword of Truth*, was in my paws! I was so excited I felt like dancing, only I didn't dare. That sword was SHARP! I didn't want to slip and cut off my tail!

Suddenly, I was overcome with emotion. Who would have thought that, I, Sir Geronimo of Stilton, could be trusted with such a powerful object? Of course, I still had work to do. I still had to cut the **LAYER OF DARKNESS** and save Blossom.

Would I be able to deliver what was expected of me? Would I be able to complete my mission? Would I be able to take off my knight boots soon? My paws were **KILLING** me!

Right then Azul put his hand on my shoulder. "Do not worry," he said. "You will be able to complete your mission. The sword will help keep you on the right path. If it is used for **EVIL** purposes, the sword will turn **RED** and feel heavy in your paw. If it is used for good purposes it will turn a sparkling blue and feel light in your paw."

PURE HEART AND SINCERE INTENTIONS

FALSE HEART AND EVIL INTENTIONS

I looked down at the sword in my paw. It was sparkling blue and didn't feel **heavy**, so I figured that was a good sign. There was only one question I still needed to ask Azul. "How will I return the sword to you when I am finished with it? I mean, will you send someone to pick it up or do I need to bring it back myself?"

The king shook his head, smiling. "No messenger service is required, Knight. The CRYSTAL SWORD, from now on, will stay with you, and it will accompany you on all your adventures in the *Kingdom of Fantasy*. It is rightfully yours, because you have demonstrated that you are worthy."

I couldn't believe it. The Crystal Sword was mine! I had never owned anything so important, so **POWERFUL**, so magical, and, well, so SHARP! I just hoped I didn't poke my eye or any other precious body part by accident!

You are worthy!

Azul took the sword and touched the tip of it to my shoulder as I KNELT before him.

"You are worthy!" he declared.

"You are worthy!" echoed the guards.

But as soon as I got up, Azul and his guards disappeared in a cloud of BLUE. Only the CRYSTAL SWORD remaining in my paw let me know it wasn't all a dream.

When I returned to my friends, Hee Haw ran up to me. "Wow! You got the Crystal Sword! Hey, can I hold it? Can I? Can I?" begged the court jester.

Webster climbed up along my arm until he reached the sword. "Ooooh, shiny . . ." he murmured, staring at it as if in a daze. "Can I climb on it? Can I? Can I?"

Before I could respond, the DRAGON OF TIME appeared by my side.

"Azul asked me to come get you," he explained. "Everybody, hop on board!"

We left immediately for the KINGDOM OF THE WITCHES. There wasn't much time — the eclipse was almost here.

We traveled all night and all day long, until finally, just before sunset, we arrived where the TOWER OF BONES had once been.

As soon as we landed, I ran toward the

DOOM DOOR. We had to save the spiders and destroy the Layer of Darkness!

But when I reached the entrance to the underground prison, I saw a small spider crying his little heart out.

Webster ran up to him and gave him a **warm** hug. The spider was his nephew **Itsy Bitsy**.

"Oh, Uncle Webster," sobbed the little spider. "The witch forced us to finish the **LAYER OF DARKNESS** and then she left with her army of

Itsy Bitsy!

Uncle Webster!

witches! She is going to destroy the kingdom with her **EVIL** plan!"

Webster patted the little spider tenderly. "It's all right," he said. "Just tell me which direction the witches flew in."

With his little leg, **Itsy** pointed to the left. "That way! I heard her say she was going to **Petrified Peak**! She was going to wait for the **ECLIPSE** and then launch the Layer of Darkness into the sky!"

Without a moment to lose, we ran off toward the peak.

As we were leaving, I heard Itsy calling after us, **"BE CAREFUL!** Eclipse and the witches are not alone. She also brought all the creatures from the **dark side of the moon**!"

To the Squeak!

We jumped on the DRAGON OF TIME, and he soared off in the direction of the **Petrified Peak**. I was so worried about the witch and the Dark Creatures, I could hardly think straight.

"To the peak!" shouted the dragon.

"To the peak!" yelled Webster.

"To the squeak! . . . I mean, the eek! . . . I mean, the p-p-place where we're g-g-going!" I stammered. Cheese niblets, I was a nervous wreck!

Soon we reached the Black Swamp and the sad River of Regret. A mountain stood out **FIERCE** against the horizon . . . Petrified Peak!

By now, night had fallen, and everything looked extra **DARK** and **spooky**. Oh, if only I had brought along a flashlight, a lantern, or my battery-operated **Cheeseball the Clown** lamp. Still, I couldn't worry about the dark now. Time was ticking, and the witch was probably getting ready to launch the Layer of Darkness.

"Hurry!" yelled Hee Haw. "We have to **STOP** her!"

The Dragon of Time beat his wings furiously, rising **HIGHER** and **HIGHER** to reach the peak.

When we got a little closer, we saw that a large crowd had gathered on the side of the mountain. It was all the creatures from the dark side of the moon!

A **lump** formed in the pit of my stomach. I felt like I had swallowed a whole block of cheddar in one gulp. The witch was so close to claiming **VICTORY**!

So, as the moon rose, we glided over Eclipse's **horrid** army . . .

STINK-SHOOTING WITCHES
LIGHTNING-BOLT WITCHES
FOUL-WATER WITCHES
STINGING-NETTLES WITCHES

CARNIVOROUS PLANTS

HAIRY BATS

WEREWOLF CHICKS

SLICING SNAKES

LITTLE GREEN MONSTERS

ASHEN PHOENIXES

ENERGY-EATING MEGA-WORMS

ABOMINABLE GIANTS

BLOCKHEAD HULKS

SEND ME UP, BIG GUY!

Eclipse flew on her broom to the top of the **Petrified Peak**. When she arrived, she strutted through the throngs of her subjects as if she were a supermodel.

Finally, she reached **Monocle**, the one-eyed king of the giants. "It's showtime!" she cackled. "Time to conquer the Kingdom of Fantasy! Send me up, big guy!"

The giant stepped **forward**. In his **ENORMOUSE** hands he held what looked like a huge paper airplane. Attached to the plane was a **DARK** fabric — it was (you guessed it!) the **LAYER OF DARKNESS**!

The giant placed the plane on the ground, and Eclipse leaped onto it.

"Are you ready, Your Wickedness?" Monocle asked the witch in a **BOOMING** voice. "Seat belt fastened, crown straightened, broom in the proper position?"

"Ready?" Eclipse screeched. "Of course, I'm ready! Now, stop asking **ridiculous questions** and **toss** this plane into the air. I will unroll the Layer of Darkness in the air and darken the *Kingdom of Fantasy* forever! Ha, ha, ha, haaa!"

Just then the sky grew a shade darker. The eclipse was starting!

"Hurry up, you fool!" the witch ordered. "What are you waiting for, a **text message** from the moon?! **TOSS ME UP!**"

"Toss her! Toss her!" the other witches and all the creatures of the dark side of the moon chanted.

Monocle raised the little airplane with the witch on top and threw it with all his might. As soon as

she took off, Eclipse **unrolled** the Layer Darkness. It stretched out like a dark blanket in the sky.

At exactly the same moment we, too, arrived at the peak of the peak — and it certainly left me petrified! But I tried to look brave.

The DRAGON OF TIME turned his body until we found ourselves face-to-face with DARKNESS. The witch waved her arms in the air triumphantly. "Oh, I'm so glad you could make it to try to be a hero, Little Mouse and friends. How charming! Now you will all get to witness my amazing victory!"

She pointed at the **LAYER OF DARKNESS**. "This is the toughest material in the entire kingdom. Nothing can destroy it!"

I took that as my cue to pull out the **Crystal Sword**.

"Are you sure **NOTHING** can destroy it?" I squeaked, doing my best to sound confident. Then I waved the sword in the air, trying desperately not to slice off my whiskers.

Immediately, Eclipse's face turned pale. Well, it was already **PALE**, but you get the idea. Her face turned even paler. "That can't be the Crystal Sword! That old peace-loving coot Azul would never part with it!" she yelled.

With a shaking paw, I lifted the sword higher so Eclipse could get a good look. "You're wrong!" I squeaked. "This is the **Crystal Sword**! Azul gave it to me because he knew I would use it to fight EVIL!"

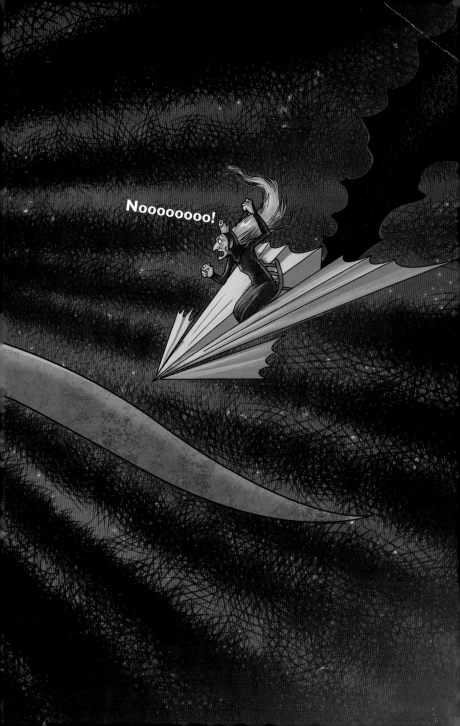

"**Let's goooo!**" I cried to the dragon. He launched himself forward and flew hard until we were under the Layer of Darkness.

At this point, the sky had turned completely **BLACK**. "Cut it! Cut it!" Hee Haw shouted in my ear.

From somewhere under me I could hear the witches' army yelling, "Don't cut it! Don't cut it!"

Of course, I already knew what to do. With one swift movement, I lifted up the Crystal Sword and sliced at the blackness, **severing** the Layer of Darkness. The dragon was right about the sword. It sliced right through that **steely** fabric like it was made of fresh cream cheese!

Swiiiiiiiisssshhhhhhh!

You'll Be Sorry Someday!

My friends let out a cheer of victory. "Woo-hoo! We did it!"

Underneath us, we could hear the disappointed **grumbling** of Eclipse's army and all the creatures of the dark side of the moon.

Meanwhile, the witch herself, who was a terribly bad sport, yelled **insults** in our direction. "This isn't the end, Rat!" she shrieked. "You'll be **sorry** someday!"

But as she was screaming, the Layer of Darkness began to fall, tumbling down into the River of Regret . . . and Eclipse **DISAPPEARED** with it. Then the moon returned to shine **brightly** in the sky. The eclipse was over, and I had succeeded at completing my mission!

The Kingdom of Fantasy was safe at last!

While the Dragon of Time flew back toward the Kingdom of the Fairies, I clutched the sword that Azul had given to me.

Who knew if Eclipse would return to **BATTLE** again? Nothing was certain. But at least I would always have my trusty CRYSTAL SWORD!

I will always have my Crystal Sword!

KNIGHT OF PEACE

We traveled for about **twenty million** days and **twenty million** nights. Well, okay, maybe it wasn't that long, but it felt like forever. I was so happy I had completed my mission, but I was very **tired**. I couldn't wait to get home to see my family and to take a nice hot cheddar BUBBLE BATH!

On and on we flew, until finally I glimpsed a light in the distance.

I blinked my eyes slowly . . .

Underneath us were the beautiful, LUSH lands of the Kingdom of the Fairies. The Dragon of Time glided SLOWLY toward the ground until I saw the steeples of Blossom's CRYSTAL CASTLE.

We landed at Dragon Airport, while the

Royal Fairy Orchestra played a welcoming serenade in honor of our return. What an honor it was to be honored!

At the entrance to the shimmering CRYSTAL CASTLE, we saw the queen. Blossom's back was to us, and we couldn't see her face. My heart hammered away under my fur so hard I felt like I would explode! Was the queen's face as youthful as it used to be? Of course, I would love her either way, wrinkles or no wrinkles. But if Blossom's face had turned smooth and young again, it meant that time had been put back on track, and that the Kingdom of Fantasy was saved!

Just when I thought I would faint from anticipation, the queen turned around. Cheesecake! She was back to her old self!

Her hair had returned to its rich turquoise color, her smile was a brilliant white, and she was

no longer leaning on a cane.

Blossom threw her arms around me in a warm embrace. "So, *Sir Geronimo of Stilton*, once again you have not only saved me but you have saved the entire Kingdom of Fantasy! How can I ever repay you?" she said, smiling kindly.

I shuffled my feet and said modestly. "Aw, it was nothing. I just had to **CLIMB** a **GINORMOUSE** rosebush, walk backward off a **steep** cliff, escape from a mad witch's lair, prove I was worthy of the magical Crystal Sword, and stop eternal darkness during a lunar **eclipse**."

The queen reached forward and placed an **oLiVe** wreath on my head. "Dear Knight," she said. "Let me offer you this simple but precious crown. I am awarding you the title **Knight of Peace**!"

Everyone cheered. And then I heard some

familiar voices arguing in the crowd. "**Me first!**" each one insisted. It was Scribblehopper, his cousin Queenie, and Little Princess Buzzy. They were arguing over who got to **hug** me first! In the end, Scribblehopper reached me first, **CRUSHING** me so hard I almost fainted.

Then someone in the crowd yelled, "Hey, when is this party going to start?"

Oof!

Knight, I thought you were a goner!

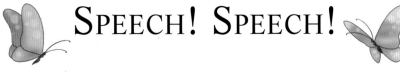

SPEECH! SPEECH!

Blossom smiled. "Now we will celebrate! My niece, Princess Precious, the guardian for all the **Winged Creatures** in the kingdom, will provide the entertainment."

A very small young fairy came forward. She had her hair in two braids and wore round

glasses just like mine. Sitting on her shoulder was the queen of the butterflies. I knew it was the queen because she wore a GLISTENING crown on her head made of tiny dewdrops.

When the princess gave a signal, an immense parade of **MULTICOLORED** butterflies appeared. They flitted all over the crystal ballroom in a spectacular and elaborate dance.

Blossom took my right paw and Princess Precious took my left, and we danced and swirled in perfect **rhythm** with the butterflies around and around the room. Well, maybe one of us wasn't in perfect rhythm. Can I help it if I have two **LEFT** paws? Still, I tried my best not to step on too many toes.

As we were dancing, I noticed Prince Lucky talking and laughing with his father, Tick Tock, the Wizard of Time.

I went over and asked, "Tick Tock, how are you?"

He smiled at me. "I am very well, thanks to you, Knight! As soon as the Wind of the West stopped **BLOWiNG**, my memory returned!"

Whew! But I still had one last **QUESTION** to ask the wizard. I had been wondering about it since the beginning of my adventure. "What is

the **TREASURE** in the Land of Time that so many travelers search for?"

The wizard smiled kindly. "My dear **Knight**, I do not reveal this **secret** to many, but you have proven that you are more than worthy, so I will tell you. In the Land of Time, there is a unique treasure of **inestimable** value. No, it is not the gold sand in the Desert of Time (though it is pretty) or my beautiful golden palace (though I love my home sweet home) or the precious **Tick Tock Timepiece** (though I must say, my invention is pretty incredible). It is something you cannot buy and is more *precious* than gold, pearls, and diamonds. Can you guess what it might be?"

I thought about the wizard's question. Suddenly, I had the answer. What could be more *precious* in the Land of Time than **TIME** itself?

I told the wizard, and he nodded. "You are

right, Knight. In fact, nothing is more precious than time. Nothing can stop it, and no one can **BUY** it!"

For a moment, I imagined what it would be like if we could **BUY** time. I pictured myself at the store purchasing a *block of time*. What would I use it for? Would I use **TEN** extra minutes before my alarm rang in the morning? (Oh, how I hate getting up in the morning!) Would I use **fifteen** extra minutes to make my breakfast? Then I might be able to whip up some of my great-grandma One Whisker's delicious **cheddar cheese** popovers. What a way to start the morning!

Or maybe I would spend the extra time with my family. I could take my nephew Benjamin to the park or go **golfing** with my grandfather William. Though I have to admit, golf isn't exactly my sport. The last time I played golf, I missed the

ball and accidentally swung my golf club into a
LAKE!

I was still thinking about **flying** golf clubs
when I realized the crowd was staring at me.
"Speech! Speech!" they shouted.

I turned **RED** with embarrassment. I'm not the
best at giving speeches, especially in front of a
large crowd. What if my paws **shook** or I started
stuttering? What if the wind blew, and a piece
of dirt got into my eye, and I started **crying**
and couldn't stop, forming a puddle at my feet,
and the **puddle** turned into a lake, and I
started to drown, and . . . well, okay, maybe that
wouldn't really happen. And, to be honest, when I
looked out at all the **SMILING** faces, I started to
relax. No one would really care if my paws shook.
Everyone just wanted to hear what I had to say.

So I smiled and said, "Ahem, my dear friends,
thank you all so much for **HONORING** me! I

ding ding dong dang ding dong dang ding dong dang ding dong dang ding dong dang ding ding dong dang ding

have learned so many things on my journey to the **LAND OF TIME**. But most of all I have learned that time is our most precious *treasure*, and we should never waste it! **Hooray for time!**"

Everyone applauded.

A warm feeling came over me as I realized I had once more helped bring **PEACE** and happiness to the Kingdom of Fantasy.

Then I heard the sound of bells.

Ding dong dang!
ing dong dang!
Ding ding!
Dong dong!
Dong dong!
ong ding!
Dong dong!

It was all the **bells** in the entire land signaling the hour. And what a magical **HOUR** it was — an hour of **PEACE** and happiness!

Then something strange happened.

The chiming bells were so **soothing** I fell asleep still standing. I was having a nice peaceful snooze when suddenly the bells grew *louder* and *louder* and *louder* and *louder* and *louder* . . .

SORRY TO WAKE YOU

I came to with a start. When I looked around, I realized I was no longer in the Kingdom of Fantasy. I was sitting in the **BLUE** pawchair in the clock shop back in New Mouse City!

Around me, all the alarm clocks in the shop were **RINGING** and buzzing and **chiming** and cuckooing! What a racket!

"Wh-what happened?!" I stammered.

In front of me, I saw the *smiling* faces of Minute Mouse and his wife, Eloise. "You fell asleep," said Eloise sweetly. "Just like your grandfather. He falls asleep when he sits in that pawchair, too. You two are so alike!"

Minute Mouse chuckled. "Sorry to wake you, Geronimo. Our clocks ring every hour on the hour!"

"It's okay. I should get going anyway," I said, waving good-bye and **STUMBLING** to the door, still in a **DAZE**.

Minute Mouse came running after me. "Wait, you forgot your watch!" he said, holding it out to me.

Oops! How could I forget my watch?! It's why I came to the **REPAIR** shop in the first place!

I put the watch up to my ear. It ticked softly in a steady rhythm. I thanked Minute Mouse and tried to pay him for the job, but he refused.

"No charge for you," he said with a smile, clapping his paw on my shoulder. "Don't forget to say hello to your grandfather!"

I thanked him again and was already through the door when I remembered something. "What was the magical secret about the Starry Rose plant?" I asked.

Minute Mouse laughed. "Oh, the secret is that it doesn't have thorns. Most rosebushes do, you know. It's not really magical. I just like to tell my customers that for fun. No one really believes me."

I BLUSHED. I guess I'm not the average customer! Then I remembered something else. "But whatever happened with the Tick Tock Timepiece?" I asked.

This time it was Eloise's turn to laugh. "Oh, Geronimo," she said with a grin. "You didn't really **believe** that story, did you? I thought you knew it was all just fantasy."

By now I had turned as **RED** as my uncle Cheesebelly's SPICY tomato sauce! "Ahem, yes, of course — well, certainly. Without a doubt, I knew it was all just a made-up story." I coughed. Was I the only mouse on the block who believed in *magic*?

I waved good-bye again and headed back toward my home sweet home. By then the sky was dark, and a full **moon** lit up the street. Ah, what a **peaceful** night!

YES, GRANDFATHER,
I DID!

As I began walking, **glistening** snowflakes began to fall. I stuck out my tongue so I could catch some. There's nothing like the taste of cold, fresh snowflakes!

With the moon **lighting** my way, I didn't even have to worry about the dark. Did I mention I'm afraid of the dark, cramped elevators, and large **BUBBLE GUM** bubbles? (A bubble once popped on me, and it took me three hours to get the gum out of my fur!)

As I walked home, I couldn't stop thinking about my adventure in the *Kingdom of Fantasy*. The whole thing was so **fresh** in my mind, and I couldn't wait to write it all down and publish it as my next book!

It was my eighth adventure in the Kingdom of Fantasy, and I would call it *The Hour of Magic*. I had learned that time was truly precious!

Finally, I arrived in front of my house.

But before I could pull out my key, **Grandfather** opened the door.

"Grandson, what are **YOU** doing here?" he said.

"Ahem, well, um, I **live** here," I squeaked, confused.

Did you come up with an idea?

Yes, I did!

Grandfather laughed. "Just teasing you!" he said, SMACKING me on the back so hard, I practically fell over. "So how did it go? Did you come up with an **IDEA** for the book?"

"Yes, Grandfather, I did! I'm going to write about the adventure I had when I went to the clock shop!" I squeaked. "I climbed up a *magical* plant, and I traveled with Scribblehopper the frog and Solitaire the knight and Princess Buzzy the bee, and I fell into a **HUMONGOUS** hourglass, and I pretended to be a **WITCH**, and . . ."

Grandfather held up his paw. "Okay, okay, Grandson. Don't give me the play-by-play. Just get writing! Your **deadline** is almost here, and I will not tolerate lateness!"

I grinned, remembering what Minute Mouse and Eloise had told me about Grandfather. He may act **TOUGH**, but deep down he was proud of me.

"I love you, Grandfather!" I squeaked.

"I love you, too, Grandson," replied Grandfather, hugging me.

Then I hugged the rest of my family, too — they were all inside, waiting for me! Ah, it felt good to be home!

Later that night, I lay in my bed, thinking again about my ADVENTURE. I had learned a lot on my trip to the Kingdom of Fantasy. From now on I would really value my **time** spent with family and friends. And of course, that meant my friends from the *Kingdom of Fantasy*, too. I had a feeling I would be seeing them again SOMEDAY. And when I do, I'll make sure to tell you all about it!

FANTASIAN ALPHABET

ABOUT THE AUTHOR

Born in New Mouse City, Mouse Island, **GERONIMO STILTON** is Rattus Emeritus of Mousomorphic Literature and of Neo-Ratonic Comparative Philosophy. For the past twenty years, he has been running *The Rodent's Gazette*, New Mouse City's most widely read daily newspaper.

Stilton was awarded the Ratitzer Prize for his scoops on *The Curse of the Cheese Pyramid* and *The Search for Sunken Treasure*. He has also received the Andersen 2000 Prize for Personality of the Year. One of his bestsellers won the 2002 eBook Award for world's best ratlings' electronic book. His works have been published all over the globe.

In his spare time, Mr. Stilton collects antique cheese rinds and plays golf. But what he most enjoys is telling stories to his nephew Benjamin.

Don't miss any of my adventures in the Kingdom of Fantasy!

THE KINGDOM OF FANTASY

THE QUEST FOR PARADISE:
THE RETURN TO THE KINGDOM OF FANTASY

THE AMAZING VOYAGE:
THE THIRD ADVENTURE IN THE KINGDOM OF FANTASY

THE DRAGON PROPHECY:
THE FOURTH ADVENTURE IN THE KINGDOM OF FANTASY

THE VOLCANO OF FIRE:
THE FIFTH ADVENTURE IN THE KINGDOM OF FANTASY

THE SEARCH FOR TREASURE:
THE SIXTH ADVENTURE IN THE KINGDOM OF FANTASY

THE ENCHANTED CHARMS:
THE SEVENTH ADVENTURE IN THE KINGDOM OF FANTASY

THE PHOENIX OF DESTINY:
AN EPIC KINGDOM OF FANTASY ADVENTURE

THE HOUR OF MAGIC:
THE EIGHTH ADVENTURE IN THE KINGDOM OF FANTASY

Be sure to read all my fabumouse adventures!

#1 Lost Treasure of the Emerald Eye

#2 The Curse of the Cheese Pyramid

#3 Cat and Mouse in a Haunted House

#4 I'm Too Fond of My Fur!

#5 Four Mice Deep in the Jungle

#6 Paws Off, Cheddarface!

#7 Red Pizzas for a Blue Count

#8 Attack of the Bandit Cats

#9 A Fabumouse Vacation for Geronimo

#10 All Because of a Cup of Coffee

#11 It's Halloween, You 'Fraidy Mouse!

#12 Merry Christmas, Geronimo!

#13 The Phantom of the Subway

#14 The Temple of the Ruby of Fire

#15 The Mona Mousa Code

#16 A Cheese-Colored Camper

#17 Watch Your Whiskers, Stilton!

#18 Shipwreck on the Pirate Islands

#19 My Name Is Stilton, Geronimo Stilton

#20 Surf's Up, Geronimo!

#21 The Wild, Wild West

#22 The Secret of Cacklefur Castle

A Christmas Tale

#23 Valentine's Day Disaster

#24 Field Trip to Niagara Falls

#25 The Search for Sunken Treasure

#26 The Mummy with No Name

#27 The Christmas Toy Factory

#28 Wedding Crasher

#29 Down and Out Down Under

#30 The Mouse Island Marathon

#31 The Mysterious Cheese Thief

Christmas Catastrophe

#32 Valley of the Giant Skeletons

#33 Geronimo and the Gold Medal Mystery

#34 Geronimo Stilton, Secret Agent

#35 A Very Merry Christmas

#36 Geronimo's Valentine

#37 The Race Across America

#38 A Fabumouse School Adventure

#39 Singing Sensation

#40 The Karate Mouse

#41 Mighty Mount Kilimanjaro

#42 The Peculiar Pumpkin Thief

#43 I'm Not a Supermouse!

#44 The Giant Diamond Robbery

#45 Save the White Whale!

#46 The Haunted Castle

#47 Run for the Hills, Geronimo!

#48 The Mystery in Venice

#49 The Way of the Samurai

#50 This Hotel Is Haunted!

#51 The Enormouse Pearl Heist

#52 Mouse in Space!

#53 Rumble in the Jungle

#54 Get into Gear, Stilton!

#55 The Golden Statue Plot

#56 Flight of the Red Bandit

The Hunt for the Golden Book

#57 The Stinky Cheese Vacation

#58 The Super Chef Contest

#59 Welcome to Moldy Manor

The Hunt for the Curious Cheese

#60 The Treasure of Easter Island

#61 Mouse House Hunter

#62 Mouse Overboard!

The Hunt for the Secret Papyrus

#63 The Cheese Experiment

#64 Magical Mission

Check out these very special editions!

**THEA STILTON:
THE JOURNEY
TO ATLANTIS**

**THEA STILTON:
THE SECRET OF
THE FAIRIES**

**THEA STILTON:
THE SECRET OF
THE SNOW**

**THEA STILTON:
THE CLOUD
CASTLE**

**THEA STILTON:
THE TREASURE
OF THE SEA**

**THE JOURNEY
THROUGH TIME**

BACK IN TIME:
THE SECOND JOURNEY
THROUGH TIME

**THE RACE
AGAINST TIME:**
THE THIRD JOURNEY
THROUGH TIME